GONEU
OF THE
RINGS

Book One of the Matchmaker Marriage Mysteries

elise sax

Gored of the Rings (Matchmaker Marriage Mysteries– Book 1) is a work of fiction. Names, characters, places, and incidents are the products of the author's imagination or are used fictitiously. Any resemblance to actual events, locales, or persons, living or dead, is entirely coincidental.

ALSO BY ELISE SAX

Matchmaker Mysteries Series

*Matchmaking Advice from Your
Grandma Zelda
Road to Matchmaker
An Affair to Dismember
Citizen Pain
The Wizards of Saws
Field of Screams*

*From Fear to Eternity
West Side Gory
Scareplane
It Happened One Fright
The Big Kill
It's a Wonderful Knife
Ship of Ghouls*

Goodnight Mysteries Series

*Die Noon
A Doom with a View
Jurassic Dark
Coal Miner's Slaughter
Wuthering Frights*

Agatha Bright Mysteries Series

*The Fear Hunter
Some Like It Shot
Fright Club
Beast of Eden
Creepy Hollow*

Matchmaker Marriage Mysteries

*Gored of the Rings
Slay Misty for Me
Scar Wars
Die Charred
Spawn with the Wind*

Partners in Crime Series

*Partners in Crime
Conspiracy in Crime
Divided in Crime*

Operation Billionaire Trilogy

*How to Marry a Billionaire
How to Marry Another Billionaire
How to Marry the Last Billionaire on Earth*

Five Wishes Series

*Going Down
Man Candy
Hot Wired
Just Sacked
Wicked Ride*

Five Wishes Series
Three More Wishes Series

*Blown Away
Inn & Out
Quick Bang
Three More Wishes Series*

For Seth, my sweet brother, who likes my books and does my taxes.

CHAPTER 1

Love is love, bubbeleh. But sometimes love wants a
party. It wants an audience, a disco band, ten bridesmaids,
and a fakakta harp. Remember to keep cool under pressure.
It's just a party. The love always shows up… I wish I could
say the same thing about the caterers. Anyway, take pleasure
in the moment because moments are gone in a blink of an
*eye. Then, **poof!** it's down to the husband and wife and a*
maxed-out credit card.

— Lesson 1, Wedding Business Advice From
Your Grandma Zelda

I dressed in jeans and a blue, sleeveless top, pulled
my long, frizzy hair into a ponytail, and went downstairs
for breakfast. It was only seven o'clock, but my grandma
Zelda was already in the kitchen. She was wearing her

blue housedress, and her hair was up in curlers. Her plastic slippers click-clacked on the linoleum floor as she walked. I watched as she put a few sliced bagels into the old gas oven.

"Why aren't you using the toaster?" I asked.

"Because your gorgeous husband fixed the toaster."

Oh. That explained it.

My name's Gladie Burger, and Grandma was right. I did have a gorgeous husband. His name was Spencer Bolton. He was the police chief, and after three years of marriage, he had decided to fix things. Even if they weren't broken.

For example, he had fixed the washing machine, the grandfather clock, and the toaster, just to name a few. Now, nothing worked.

"Dolly, we can't wash our clothes, I have no idea what time it is, and now I have to toast my bagels in the oven. But I still like to look at Spencer's tushy. Not in a creepy way. In a considerate, approving way."

"Me, too," I said. Grandma only got to look at Spencer's ass fully clothed, though, whereas I got to see it in all its glory whenever I wanted to. It had a lot of glory.

Spencer and I lived with my grandmother in her large Victorian house in Cannes, California. Our small town had a small population of a couple thousand people, but each of those people made a lot of noise. We were nestled in the mountains east of San Diego, and we were a tourist destination for those looking for apple pie and antiques.

Cannes was founded in the late 1800s after gold was discovered here, but the mine dried up pretty quickly. Most of the people left after that, but some—like my great grandparents—decided to stay on.

Opening the refrigerator, I took out the orange juice, eggs, and cream cheese.

"It's going to be dry today," Grandma told me, taking the toasted bagels out of the oven.

She had a way of knowing things that couldn't be known, but I had the same way. We both had the gift, a third eye that was very handy for weather and making love matches. My gift used to be on fire, but it had calmed down to a dull roar.

"I know. I put Chapstick in my purse. I have to meet Susan Bass at noon to go over final details."

Grandma sighed but smiled at me encouragingly, with some effort. I had decided to branch out from our matchmaking business and go into weddings. Grandma patted my shoulder and sat across from me at the kitchen table, which she had bought in 1958.

"I support your efforts to be happy," she said. She slathered cream cheese on a bagel and took a bite.

I poured coffee into a cup and added whole milk. "I *am* happy," I insisted. "I just need something to spice up my life."

"Did I hear my name being called, Pinky?" Spencer asked, walking into the kitchen.

I sucked in air, and my heart raced. After three years of marriage, just the sight of Spencer could get me going. He was something to behold in his Armani suit. His thick dark hair was purposely slightly mussed, and he had a perfect five o'clock shadow happening at seven o'clock in the morning on his beautiful face that made me want to jump all over him, even though I had just done that in the shower only a few minutes before.

He winked at me with one of his blue eyes and draped his jacket over a chair.

"Gladie was just telling me that she's happy," Grandma told him.

Spencer put on his "kiss the cook" apron and slapped a frying pan onto the stove. Every morning, he was in charge of the eggs. Either over easy, scrambled, or an omelet, he was a whizz with an egg and a spatula.

"You can thank me for that," Spencer boasted. "I aim to please, and I'm very generous with the happy endings."

He winked at me and smirked his usual little smirk.

"He's such a darling," Grandma gushed.

"He's five years old," I chastised, but I felt myself blush, and I hid my face with my cup, as I took a sip.

Spencer whipped an omelet together with smoked salmon. "Another beautiful day in paradise," he mused, as happy as a clam. "Quiet. Peaceful. No cult leaders. No flying donkeys. No one dropping dead. Not even one dead body in a refrigerator, a trash can, or a lobster tank. Have you noticed that? Nobody's been murdered in a long time."

"Not for three years," I said, trying to keep my voice light.

Spencer waved his spatula at me like he was conducting a symphony. "You know what? I think you're right. Three years."

"Not since you were married," Grandma said.

She and I locked eyes for a split second, and in that instant, I knew that she knew what I had kept hidden for so long.

I was jonesing for a nice murder to solve.

Here's the thing: In the first year that I had moved back to Cannes to help with Grandma's matchmaking business, I had stumbled on more dead bodies than the coroner at the morgue. I had solved loads of murders, and I had gotten the reputation of a sort of Miss Marple in town.

Then, along with marital bliss, came a lull in the local murders. In fact, there hadn't been one since after my honeymoon. Nothing. Bupkis.

Not that I hoped someone would get murdered, but c'mon! Without a murder to solve, I didn't feel quite…like me.

Spencer dished out the omelet and took a seat next to me. "You're right," he said with his mouth full. "Look at that, Pinky. You're good luck for me. My days are peaceful and tranquil. Yesterday, our biggest law enforcement activity was giving Ruth Fletcher a jaywalking ticket."

Grandma laughed. "I would have loved to see that."

Ruth was an ornery eighty-eight-year-old woman who owned the local tea shop.

"She kneed Remington in the balls, but he laughed it off," Spencer said about one of his two detectives. Remington had left town a few years ago but came back a few months later. He and I had had a thing once upon a time, but it was long forgotten.

"Remington has strong balls," Grandma agreed.

Spencer took a bite of a bagel. "You know what? Come to think of it, not only do we not have murders here anymore, but for the most part, the crazy has left the town." He kissed me lightly on the lips. "That must be your influence," he said, generously. "You want me to wash up?"

I shook my head. "No, you head on to work. Grandma and I are still eating."

He smiled wide and kissed me again, like he was the happiest married man in America. And maybe he was.

After he left, Grandma made a point of staring me down. I knew that look. It was the look she gave me when she wanted me to spill the beans.

"No beans," I said. "I have absolutely no beans. I'm happy. And there's no crazy in the town, and killers are taking a much-needed vacation. Or a sabbatical. Or the bastards have up and retired."

My voice raised at the end of my statement about killers, and I clamped my lips together.

"We got any Entenmann's Danish?" I asked and got up. I riffled through the pantry, but couldn't find them.

Grandma joined me in the pantry. "Entenmann's stopped making them."

I blinked at her, unsure if I had heard her correctly. "What?"

"And the coffee cake, too. Entenmann's is in the doughnut business now."

I stepped back in shock and my shoulders knocked into the shelves. "What? Is this April Fools?"

"No. It's August."

"Why do we need Entenmann's to make doughnuts? That's Krispy Kreme's job. And now Walley's sells Krispy Kreme doughnut holes. Entenmann's job is to make Danish and coffee cake. Danish and coffee cake!" My voice cracked, and I clutched at my throat.

"There's Sara Lee in the freezer," Grandma offered.

"The world has gone crazy," I continued in a tirade. "Nobody's doing what they're supposed to be doing."

I took a deep breath and tried to calm down. It was no use. I was het up, but good.

"I'm going to Tea Time for a latte," I announced.

"You go ahead. Meryl's stopping by for breakfast. We'll clean up later."

I grabbed my purse and walked out the front door. A dry wind hit me in the face. We had had a mild August so far, but today was hot and dry, and I knew it was going to last like this for at least a week.

I walked down the steep driveway, past Grandma's rosebushes. Across the street, workers were arriving. About a year ago, the famous artist Pablo Cohen had bought the house from Spencer and me and had renovated it from top to bottom. Now, he was focusing on the outside, enlarging the pool and building a pool house.

Pablo had moved here from New York, and he was not concerned about the general belief in town that his house was cursed. So far, he had been right. He had lived happily there since he had moved in, and his career continued to thrive.

Turning right, I walked a couple blocks and turned left onto Main Street toward Tea Time.

Despite the name, Tea Time made the best lattes in Cannes. The shop used to be a saloon during the Wild West days, and there were still a couple bullet holes in a wall, but now it was all about tea, headed by Ruth, it's dictatorial owner.

I opened the door and walked in. There were two other people in the shop, drinking tea and eating scones at different tables. I slapped my credit card on the counter, which was the saloon's original bar. Ruth stood behind it in men's slacks and a starched button-down shirt.

"Latte, Ruth. And make it a double."

Her eyes flicked to my card and back up to my face.

"You sure play fast and loose with that card these days. Must be nice to be a kept woman."

"I'm married, Ruth. I'm not kept. Kept women

don't start wedding businesses. Kept women don't clean toilets."

Ruth scowled, pulling her lips tight into a straight line.

"I give the wedding thing two weeks, tops. Come back to reality, girl. You're not froufrou. All of that taffeta's going to make you barking mad."

"Take that back, Ruth. I am froufrou."

She waved dismissively at me. "Look at you. Jeans and a shirt. You wouldn't catch Lucy wearing jeans and a shirt."

Lucy was one of my best friends. She was a Southern Belle with impeccable style. I had never seen her wear anything but a dress.

"Lucy doesn't own jeans and a shirt," I said.

"Exactly my point."

I laid my forehead on the counter in defeat. "Ruth, please. Coffee," I said into the polished wood. "Don't make it so hard. I need caffeine. Entenmann's stopped making Danish, and I have a meeting with Susan Bass to go over last-minute details. It's my first wedding job, and the wedding is this Saturday."

Ruth harrumphed. "In four days? Susan Bass? In that case, I see your new business lasting until Sunday. Susan is a piece of work. I still remember her high school graduation party. The mayor had to be airlifted to the closest trauma center because of an incident involving a hatchet and a Teletubby."

"Latte," I moaned.

"Keep your shirt on, Il Duce," she said and turned toward the espresso machine.

I stood up straight. "Do you have anything that resembles an Entenmann's Danish?"

"No, but I've got *good* cherry Danish that I made this morning."

"Perfect. Give me two. No, on second thought, give me three."

I sat at a table, and a couple minutes later Ruth brought me my order. Then, she brought over a pot of tea and sat with me.

"A three-Danish day, huh?" Ruth asked. "Trouble in paradise, or was I right about your new business?"

She wasn't right on either score, but I was having my share of three-Danish days, lately.

Ruth poured herself a cup of tea and nodded wisely, like she had just finished reading my thoughts, which were written on my shirt in neon pink raised lettering.

"In my day, we would have called what you have as melancholia," she told me.

"What day was that? Was Nero fiddling on that

day?"

"You sure talk a lot of sass toward the woman who touches your food."

She had a point.

"Sorry. Tell me more about melancholia."

"It's what women got when they realized they were doomed to a life of drudgery."

"I'm not a drudge, Ruth. I don't even do my own laundry. Besides, I'm a businesswoman with a credit card."

Ruth barked a laugh. "A credit card that your husband had to co-sign."

That was true. My bad credit had been so bad that it had followed me into marriage.

"That's a lie," I lied.

"Yeah, right. Anyway, you better be careful about melancholia. The only cure is being yourself. You remember what that is, right? Yourself? Or maybe you've forgotten who you are."

She was getting much too close for comfort, so I bit into a Danish and chewed.

Ruth rubbed her hands. "Damned hands. All of a sudden a week ago, they started acting up."

I sat up straight. "Maybe it's arsenic," I suggested with more than a twinge of hope in my voice.

Ruth slapped the side of my head. "Would you

stop hoping that everyone with an ailment is being poisoned? It's unseemly."

I hung my head in shame. "Sorry."

"Nobody's been poisoned in this town since you got married."

"I know."

"Crazy girl, wanting folks to be poisoned. I have enough to deal with, with the headache from next door."

The shop next door had been empty for a long time, but someone had leased it and workers had been going in and out of it for weeks, making a lot of noise and a huge mess.

"Any idea yet what's going in next door?" I asked.

"Not a clue. It's all been very hush-hush, but a woman owns the business, whatever it is."

After I left Tea Time, I walked home to pick up my car. Pablo was giving instructions to his workers across the street, and he waved at me in a neighborly way. I waved back and turned into our driveway.

With Pablo's renovation and the new whatever that was opening next to Tea Time, Cannes looked like it was booming. I didn't know if that was a good thing or a bad thing. I loved our small-town vibe, but an influx of new people might mean more weddings for my new business.

A handful of women of different ages passed me on their way to the front door for the Second Chancers Singles meeting. Grandma stepped out and gestured toward me.

"Don't forget to pick up the ointment for my bunions at the pharmacy," she called. "The prescription is ready. And while you're there, pick up a box of the wart treatment that I like so much. We're out, and you never know when I need to dole it out."

"Sure thing, Grandma," I called back.

I got into my silver Oldsmobile Cutlass Supreme and backed down the driveway. I still had plenty of time before my meeting, so I decided to take a little drive. Because of the dry, hot weather, I cranked up the car's AC and drove out of the Historic District where we lived, toward Lake Indian Springs. It was a beautiful day without a cloud in the sky. And it was quiet.

Very, very quiet.

Just like always.

I didn't make it to the lake, though. Ahead of me was Cannes Center Park, and across the way from that was Burger Boy. They had recently expanded their full menu hours, and since there was still no Entenmann's in my stomach, I thought their triple patty bacon cheeseburger would hit the spot. Especially if I got fries, too.

No, I didn't make a habit of eating that way every day. All right…Yes, I did make a habit of eating like that every day, but not as *much of it* every day. It didn't take Freud to figure out that I was trying to fill a hole that even Spencer's beautiful doodah couldn't fill.

"I'll have the triple patty bacon cheeseburger, please," I shouted into the plastic Burger Boy's mouth in the drive-thru.

"Will that complete your order?"

"Yes. I mean, no. Fries. I need fries, too."

"We have a new Burger Boy Larger Than Life size. Would you like that?"

"Yes. My dog really likes fries."

I didn't have a dog, but I didn't want the plastic Burger Boy to know that I was eating Burger Boy Larger Than Life Size fries at ten in the morning.

I paid at the window, and they handed me my bag of food. I drove around to the parking lot and stopped for a moment to shove some fries into my mouth and to partially unwrap the cheeseburger so I could eat it while I drove.

As I unwrapped, the Burger Boy door opened, and four skateboarders rolled out. I had dealt with them in the past. Marijuana had done a number on their brain cells, but they were nice guys.

One of them, who was dressed in board shorts

and no shirt, waved to me like he wanted to talk to me, and I opened my window.

"Hey, it's the babe," another skateboarder announced.

"Cool. The babe," another one repeated.

"Yeah, cool."

"So cool."

"Babe. Cool."

They sounded like a drug-addled singing group. I knew that they could go on like that for a while, so I interrupted. "What's up?" I asked the no-shirted skateboarder. He was sort of their leader.

He showed me an insulated bag he was carrying.

"I'm a delivery guy these days," he said with pride.

"Congratulations."

He stuck his hand in the bag and pulled out some fries. He plopped them into his open mouth and then another guy did the same thing.

"Are you supposed to be doing that?" I asked. "Isn't that the customer's food?"

"Yeah, but we only take about twenty percent. That's kinda expected."

"Yeah, expected," another skateboarder said.

"Yeah, like if they get the ten-piece meal deal at Chick'n Lik'n, we eat two pieces," the lead skateboarder explained.

Chick'n Lik'n sounded good. Maybe I would get that for lunch. I could bring it back for Grandma to share so I wouldn't look as bad.

"Those are good math skills," I complimented him.

He shrugged. "In my previous line of work, I had to know percentages."

"And grams," another skateboarder said. "He knows all about grams."

"Cool," I said. Oh, no. They were contagious.

"Yeah, cool."

"Totally cool."

"Cool and bitchin'."

"Well, see ya, babe," the head skateboarder said. He kicked off across the parking lot.

"See ya, babe."

"Bye, babe."

"Later, babe."

I took a big bite of my cheeseburger as I watched them skateboard away. I also made a mental note to never order any food to be delivered.

Pulling out of the parking lot, I drove back to the Historic District and parked in front of the pharmacy.

Normally, I would have snagged a box of Pop-Tarts and a six-pack of root beer while I was in the store, but this time, since I was already eating from a Burger Boy bag that I was carrying with me, I went straight for the long prescription line.

The mayor came in and stood behind me in line. "I'm going to visit your grandmother after I pick up Dulcinea's anti-anxiety medicine," he told me.

Dulcinea was his donkey. He had sent her off to Colorado but brought her back to Cannes when he grew too lonely. Ever since she had flown over the town, she had anxiety issues.

I took a bite of my cheeseburger. "Oh, yeah? More meetings about Star Fest?"

He shook his head. "No. We've got that pretty locked up. I've got something else special planned that is going to knock Cannes on its ear."

"Is that good? It sounds like it would hurt."

"No dumber man has ever walked the earth," I heard Meryl, the blue-haired librarian, mutter under her breath in front of me. She was right. The mayor was dumber than steamed spinach.

"Hurry this line up!" Lou the auto mechanic yelled behind the mayor. "I need my cholesterol medicine pronto. There's a carburetor waiting for me."

"Never hurry a pharmacist," the pharmacist yelled back at Lou. "Otherwise, I'll lose count of the pills. Oh, damn it. Where was I? One, two, three…"

I shoved a handful of fries into my mouth. The line moved forward at a snail's pace. I continued eating as I heard the others in line recite a litany of everything that can go wrong with the human body.

Finally, I reached the front.

"I'm here to pick up my grandmother's bunion ointment," I told the pharmacist. "And do you have any of the wart stuff she likes?"

"I don't know," he said and pushed a button on the microphone that sat on the counter. "Dot! Dot!" he barked into the microphone. The sound bounced off the walls and blared through the store. "Dot! Gladie Burger's got warts."

"No, I don't," I insisted.

"Do you have the wart kit handy for Gladie's warts?" the pharmacist bellowed.

"Do you really have to use the microphone?" I pleaded.

"We've got two kinds!" Dot hollered back from an aisle. "Where're your warts, Gladie? You got big ones? Is it some place private? We've got a kit for that, too."

Everyone in line stared at me, waiting, I assumed, to find out if I had warts in my private place. I put more French fries in my mouth.

"Bring up the stuff for genital warts, Dot," the pharmacist barked into the microphone. It sounded even louder now, if that was possible. "Gladie turned red when you said genital warts, so I think that's what she's got."

"That old hound dog Spencer," Lou commented. "If you had picked me instead of him, you would be all clean down in your hoochie vajayjay."

I grabbed the microphone from the pharmacist and pushed the button.

"Attention," I shouted into it. The microphone complained with a loud screeching noise, but I continued. "I do *not* have genital warts. I repeat: I do *not* have genital warts. Dot, step away from the genital warts kit. My hoochie vajayjay is clean as a whistle."

Just then, the door opened, and a giant chicken walked in.

Not a *giant* giant. It was average man-sized. But it was giant for a chicken.

"This is a stickup," the chicken announced and held up a gun with one of its wings.

"Now, there's something you don't see every day," the pharmacist noted. "Dammit. I lost count, again."

CHAPTER 2

Always expect the unexpected, bubbeleh. Weddings are like that. Parties are bad enough, but parties that mean more to the hosts than breathing, toilet paper, or world peace mean that every little hiccough in the works is going to be traumatic. So, go with the flow. Never let them see you sweat. Remember that every fakakta problem is just a solution in disguise. And always have baby wipes with you. They fix everything.

— Lesson 2, Wedding Business Advice From
Your Grandma Zelda

"Hands up!" The chicken bellowed.

He had a gravelly voice, like a chain smoker, and he walked with a slight limp, all the while aiming his gun in our general direction.

"Now see here, my good man," the mayor started.

"Shut up, or I'll fill you full of holes," the chicken growled.

I chastised myself for hoping that he would kill the mayor, and then I would solve his murder, figure out who the chicken was, and bring him to justice. Geez. I really needed help. Was there a Miss Marple Anonymous meeting I could go to?

"I can't put my hands up," Meryl complained. "I have bursitis in my shoulder."

The chicken wiped at his mask with the back of his wing. It was a very dry day, and I bet he was broiling in his costume. I chuckled at the thought of the chicken broiling.

"Shut up!" the chicken yelled. He waved his gun at me. My hands shot up in the air, and fries flew everywhere. Now, I really would have to stop at Chik'n Lik'n. In fact, the chicken's costume looked awfully similar to the guy they used to hold up a sign. What was his name? Did he have a limp? Could he have decided to hold up the pharmacy during his lunch hour?

The pharmacist pushed some buttons on the cash register and pulled out all of the cash.

"Here. This is all we got," he said, extending his

hand toward the chicken.

"I don't want your cash," the chicken spat.

"Too right, chicken," the mayor said. "Cash is clumsy, old-fashioned, and it carries more germs than the toilet seat. I'm going to fix all that."

Meryl slapped her forehead.

"Hurry this up," Lou urged. "I have a carburetor waiting for me."

"Give me the pills," the chicken ordered the pharmacist.

"Which pills?" The pharmacist asked.

"Not my cholesterol pills," Lou warned.

"Not my blood pressure medicine," the mayor pleaded.

"I hope he doesn't take your vaginal wart medicine," Dot said, appearing at my side.

I let my hands drop. "Once again, I do not have vaginal warts."

"Don't take her vaginal warts medicine," the pharmacist asked the chicken.

But the chicken didn't have vaginal warts, either, or if he did, he didn't care about them because he only wanted opioids.

"Dammit. That was my medicine," Meryl complained. "For my bursitis," she added.

The pharmacist handed the chicken the pills.

"Don't try anything," the chicken warned us and waved his gun around like he was ushering a plane into a terminal. He didn't need to worry. I wasn't going to try anything except for the new Polynesian sauce at Chik'n Lik'n right after I got Grandma her prescription.

But Meryl had other ideas. I guess the idea of an un-medicated bursitis flare-up made her want to try all kinds of things. As the chicken made his way past us, Meryl let out a chilling scream and karate chopped him right on his beak. One of the bottles of opioids flew out of his wings, and he flapped like crazy to catch it.

After he caught his stolen goods, he swatted Meryl with the back of his wing, and she went down hard on the 1950s-era linoleum floor.

That's when the smart part of my brain shut off, and the crazy, stupid part whirred into action.

It wasn't the first time that my brain had decided to act that way. Before I got married, my brain was more or less caught in the crazy stupid gear.

"How dare you!" I exclaimed, sounding like I was a school matron in an old film. The chicken didn't take any notice of me. He kept walking toward the door with his pills. I flung myself onto his back and wrapped my limbs around him.

"Stop in the name of the law!" I cried.

"Get off me!" he yelled and tried to shrug me off.

It didn't work. I held on tight, like I was a rodeo star on a bucking bronco.

"Stop! Are you crazy? I have a gun!" He said and waved it around again, this time like he was a baton twirler in a parade. That's when I noticed that his gun wasn't real.

"The gun is chocolate," I announced.

"It's not. It's licorice," the chicken retorted.

Blech. I can't stand black licorice.

I planted my hands over his eyes and pulled his head back. The chicken swatted at me, but he was off-balance. He stumbled into the shampoo shelf, spun around, and ran into the deodorant section. Somehow, though, he managed to stay upright. He staggered out of the personal hygiene aisle and into the family-planning aisle. Boxes of condoms went everywhere, but somehow, he managed to sidestep them as he tried to free his eyes from my hands.

He wasn't successful. He didn't see a box of two lavender-scented douches, and he went over like a tree, but in slow motion, sidestepping a dozen times. Finally, he fell off his feet with me on top of him, right on top of the blood pressure machine that customers could use for free.

The chicken and I struggled against each other. He was a lot bigger and stronger than I was, but I had hands instead of wings, and that was a definite plus. His stolen pills fell to the floor.

"Dammit," the chicken muttered and swatted me with his licorice gun. It turned out that black licorice not only tasted disgusting, but it also hurt.

And that's when it happened.

"Are you kidding me?"

"It's not my fault."

Spencer stood over me with his hands on his Armani-clad hips and his mouth wide open in shock. I didn't blame him. I was in shock, too.

Meryl took a picture of me with her phone.

"What do you think you're doing?" Spencer demanded.

She took another photo. "I've been trying to get more followers on Instagram. This should do it."

Lou had left the pharmacy but returned with the jaws of life that he kept in his truck.

"What the hell do you think you're going to do with *that*?" The pharmacist asked.

"How else do you expect to get her head out of there?" Lou demanded.

"The blood pressure machine is a lease. I'm not going to pay for a new one. You know how much these things cost?" the pharmacist demanded.

It was a nice blood pressure machine, from what I could tell. It had an attached stool to sit on, and a sturdy cuff with fancy buttons next to it on a large screen. I wasn't using it right, though. For one, I was kneeling on the stool. And second, instead of my arm, my head had gone through the cuff and gotten stuck there.

I didn't know how it happened. My head must've been twice the circumference of the pressure cuff, but the chicken and I had scuffled pretty hard, and sometimes laws of physics don't apply to me. Now I was stuck like a dog in a too-tight collar. And the chicken was long gone, probably partying somewhere with his ill-gotten narcotics.

"Stop taking pictures, Meryl," Spencer growled. "You're not going to put my wife on your Instagram page."

Meryl stuck her tongue out at him, but she dutifully put her phone back in her purse. "Big talker," she complained. "At least I didn't give her vaginal warts."

Spencer blinked. "What?"

"She has a point," Lou said.

The pharmacist patted Spencer's back. "We've all been there man."

Spencer shrugged him off. "What the hell's going on here? I was having a great, quiet day. I was having a great, quiet three years." He leaned over so our faces were nearly touching. "This better be an aberration, Pinky. I like quiet."

"I'm sure this is a blip," I assured him.

Lou approached me with the jaws of life.

"No way," the pharmacist cried. "Don't damage the machine."

"How else are we going to get her out of there?" Lou asked.

"Maybe she can stay there for a day or two," I heard the mayor say. He must've been behind me. "That way, she'll lose weight and her head will shrink."

This suggestion was met with a long silence, but I could've sworn I heard Meryl's teeth grinding together. And after a minute, Spencer chuckled into his hand.

"Maybe we can grease her down," the pharmacist suggested. "Dot! Dot! give me some Crisco from aisle four."

One minute a chicken was waving a gun at me, and the next minute, men were going to slather Crisco all over me. I was definitely going to need Chik'n Lik'n.

Just when I thought it couldn't get any worse, Ruth came in to do her daily blood pressure check.

"What the hell is this?" she demanded. "Stop playing around, girl. I need to check my blood pressure. I'm older than dirt, you know. I'm one blood pressure spike away from keeling over, and then you'd never drink another latte again."

"That's good enough for me," the pharmacist said. "Crisco it is."

Dot brought the Crisco, and Meryl greased my neck and head. It worked. My head slipped out of the blood pressure machine, and I was finally free.

"That's it. You're coming with me," Spencer told me.

"What're you talking about?" I asked.

"I don't want you to get into any trouble."

I put my hands on my hips and stomped my foot. A chunk of Crisco flew off my hair and landed on Spencer's suit jacket. He cried out and ran to aisle two, where there were swimming noodles and beach towels for sale. I followed him and watched him dab at his suit with a towel, but it didn't help the grease stain.

"I'm a grown woman. I don't get into trouble," I insisted.

"Not for three years. I'll grant you that, but I want to make sure that doesn't change."

"I have an appointment at two o'clock with my client."

"That's three hours from now."

"Fine, but you're buying me Chik'n Lik'n. I haven't eaten all day," I lied. "And Pop- Tarts. I need Pop-Tarts."

Spencer bought a towel, two boxes of S'Mores Pop-Tarts, and a six-pack of root beer. Spencer's detective, Remington, came in to interview the witnesses, and he winked at me, making me blush. Spencer noticed, and he slipped a territorial arm around me, which further stained his suit.

There had been no sign of the chicken and no clue about his identity.

He had flown the coop.

Outside, Spencer handed me a box of Pop-Tarts, and I ripped it open. A piece of cardboard fell to the ground, and I bent down to pick it up. Next to it was a little white pill. I sucked in air.

"Spencer, look at this."

I pointed at the ground. He crouched down and inspected the pill.

"Opioid," he said. "That can't be a coincidence."

"Look, there's another one," I said pointing to a spot about a foot up the street. The chicken must've dropped his pills. "And there's another one up there. And another one."

"The chicken left an opioid trail," Spencer muttered under his breath "Oh, shit. Did I just say that? Hand me a Pop-Tart."

Reluctantly, I handed him one of the tin foil packets. We both took a large bite of our Pop-Tarts.

"Okay, I'm ready now," Spencer said. "Let's follow the white pill road to the chicken."

It was an easy trail to follow. The chicken had left behind a pill every foot or so.

Spencer took his gun out of his shoulder holster. "Pinky, you stay here."

"Uh… No."

He sighed and looked up at the clear blue sky. "At least promise me you'll stay behind me."

"May I have the rest of the Pop-Tarts?"

"But they're S'Mores," Spencer whined. "That's my favorite kind."

"Okay, you can have another foil packet, but the rest are mine."

"Deal," he said. He tried to shake my hand, but my hands were full of Pop-Tarts.

He dropped his bag on the ground and held his gun with both hands.

He skulked carefully up the streets, following the trail. He looked very sexy when he skulked. He skulked just like a superhero. My lower half pulsed with sudden need, but I didn't want to interfere with justice by jumping all over Spencer. I took another bite of my Pop-Tart.

He turned his head and gestured to a small side street. The trail of pills ended there. Spencer turned into the street, and I followed right behind.

Up ahead, the chicken was slumped on the ground, leaning against a dumpster. He had taken his head off, revealing a normal middle-aged guy with adult acne. He was staring into space, and he looked like he was feeling no pain.

Spencer stood over him. "You're under arrest, chicken."

The chicken blinked a few times, as if he was trying to focus. I would've bet good money that he wouldn't be successful at focusing.

"But I have glaucoma, dude," he told Spencer.

"That's for marijuana, genius, which is legal now, by the way."

"I meant I have a bad knee. That's what I meant," he corrected.

Spencer pulled the chicken up and cuffed one of his wings. "I'm cuffing a chicken," he said to no one in particular, as if he didn't believe it himself.

As part of a theme, we stopped at Chik'n Lik'n on our way to the police station. The chicken was in the backseat, high as a kite.

It wasn't until we got to the station that Spencer realized that we had forgotten to put the towel on my seat, and now the headrest looked like it had been soaked in a vat of oil.

"This is turning out to be a great day," Spencer growled.

Spencer took the chicken inside, while I carried the groceries and the other chicken in.

Fred Lytton was the desk sergeant, and he greeted me when I walked inside. "Hello, Underwear Girl," he gushed. "Gosh, you look awfully pretty today. I like your new hairstyle. Very sleek."

Fred called me Underwear Girl after an unfortunate incident, which ended with me flashing my pink underpants to a large section of the town. It had happened years ago, but it had made quite an impression. It was the reason that Spencer called me Pinky.

I took the food back to Spencer's office. Even though we lived in a tiny town, the police station was only a few years old, and it was state-of-the-art with fake marble floors and beautiful furnishings. Spencer's office was no different.

I laid the chicken and root beer out on Spencer's desk and scooped a spoonful of mashed potatoes into my mouth. Then I sat and began to chow down.

I got through two thighs, a biscuit, and the entire container of mashed potatoes. I unbuttoned my jeans and sat back in the chair. My anxiety was down. I felt both sedated and gross with fast food bloat. Spencer came in and stared at the Chik'n Lik'n aftermath.

"Impressive," he noted and sat behind his desk. "You have quite an appetite lately. You'd tell me if you had news, right?"

He meant, news if I was pregnant. We had been very careful not to talk about babies during our marriage. I was pretty sure that Spencer would be delighted to have a whole baseball team worth of little Spencer's walking around, but I was diligent about taking the pill every evening after I brushed my teeth. It wasn't that I didn't like children. I loved being an auntie to my two best friends' children, but the idea of being in charge of my own little humans filled me with dread. After all, I had no idea how to make healthy snacks. I knew it had something to do with cutting up vegetables, and no good could come of that.

"I'm as regular as a Swiss watch," I told Spencer.

I didn't know if his face showed relief or disappointment. He grabbed the rest of the Chik'n Lik'n, as if he was afraid that I was going to eat it all before he got a bite.

"Don't forget that I'm going out with Lucy and Bridget," I told him. Now that I was married and my friends became mothers, we didn't spend as much time together as we used to, but we still saw each other most days and did a girls night out once a week.

Spencer took a big bite of his chicken. "I haven't

forgotten. Harry set up a poker game for tonight. Don't look at me that way."

"I'm not looking at you that way," I lied. I was totally looking at him that way.

"Don't lose your shirt, again," I added.

"I only lost it that one time."

"I mean, you also lost three-hundred-dollars, but you came home without your shirt."

Spencer waggled his eyebrows and smirked his little smirk. "You still like to see me without a shirt."

I felt myself blush, like I was a Christmas tree, and someone had just turned on the lights.

Spencer's eyes grew dark, and I knew that we were two seconds away from having hot sweaty snuggle bunnies on his desk. Again.

"I like seeing you without a shirt," I agreed with a croak. Spencer without a shirt was a sight to behold. He wasn't as muscular as Remington, but every square inch of him was Grade A prime. "But I don't like to think of Uncle Harry wearing your shirt."

Uncle Harry wasn't my uncle, but he liked to be called uncle, and he was married to Lucy. He was about five-foot-three and he had no neck, but he was Prince Charming to Lucy.

Spencer laughed. "Like Harry could ever fit into my shirt."

His eyes grew even darker, and he got up and walked around the desk to my side. Sitting on the edge, he drew my knees between his legs and ran a strong hand up my thigh.

I bit my lip and try to catch my breath. Oh my God, this was really going to happen. Spencer made desk sex really good. It was almost as good as shower sex and way better than car sex.

"That Crisco in your hair is starting to work for me," he said. His hand had reached the top of my thigh and was taking a detour in. Oh, I loved detours.

"It's not just in my hair. It's down my neck and back. I feel like a Toyota that's just been to the Lube and Tube."

"Stop talking sexy to me, Pinky, or I'm going to blow right here before we ever get started."

"Blow," I repeated. "Now you're talking sexy."

The door opened, and Officer James stuck his head in. "Dead body on Orchard Way up in the apple orchard, Chief," he said. "Looks like murder."

"Murder?" I cried, jumping up. "Oh, goody!"

CHAPTER 3

Sometimes things aren't what they seem. Sometimes brides don't want what they say they want. Have you noticed that, dolly? Have you noticed how folks say they want this and that and then this and that some more? But when they get this and that, they feel empty? They want it so bad that they're willing to do everything to get it, like a thirty-thousand-dollar ice sculpture. Some people want that. But ice sculptures melt, and the thirty-thousand-dollars melts along with it. Think about that, bubbeleh. Don't focus on the things that melt. Look behind the want. Look at what's real.

— Lesson 3, Wedding Business Advice From Your Grandma Zelda

"Oh, goody?"

"It's a natural reaction, Spencer. Keep your eyes on the road."

"Oh, goody?"

I fiddled with some of the buttons on the dashboard. "We need to step it up. How do I put the siren on?"

Spencer slapped my hand away. "Oh, goody?"

"Hurry up! The murderer is going to get away." A soft giggle escaped my lips.

"I can't believe I agreed to take you to the scene," he grumbled.

"You had to agree. I *made* you agree."

Spencer ran a hand over his hair. "You blackmailed me. You said I could never do the thing I like to do to you, again."

"That's right. And just so we're clear, I was talking about the thing you already do to me every Saturday morning. I still won't let you do the other thing."

"I really want to do the other thing."

"I know. You've made that perfectly clear. I would have to be dead to let you do that other thing to me. And not still warm kind of dead. Cold and rotting away kind of dead."

We easily found the scene of the crime in the

orchards. Sergeant Brody had taped off the area. Spencer parked on the side of the road, right behind the bloody corpse of a woman.

Spencer turned off the car and shot me a puppy dog look. "What're the odds of getting you to stay in the car?"

"Great odds, if you never want to do the thing again."

"You're a hard woman, Pinky."

We got out of the car and stood over the woman.

"We got a call about fifteen minutes ago from a motorist, Chief," Sergeant Brody explained. "I haven't touched the body. She's obviously gone, so I'm waiting for Remington to do the forensics."

"Good work," Spencer told him.

The sergeant was right. The woman was obviously gone. She was lying on her stomach, and the back of her head was covered in blood. She was naked, and I didn't want to think about how she had suffered. Suddenly, I felt horrible about my *oh, goody* reaction.

There was a sound in the trees behind me, and I whipped around. I had once had an interaction with the bear in the orchards, and I didn't want to replicate that. But there was no bear. I heard another sound, and I squinted, but all I could see were apple trees.

"Call in the coroner," Spencer told Brody. Then,

he pointed at me. "What did you do?"

I touched my chest. "Me? Nothing. What do you mean? Are you accusing me of killing that girl?"

"No, I'm accusing you of messing with the molecules in the air."

"Is that a euphemism for farting?" I asked. "Because it's unfair to expect me to eat three scones, the larger-than-life meal deal at Burger Boy, a box of Pop-Tarts, and the number three at Chik'n Lik'n and not fart. And besides, we're outside in the wilderness, and farting is allowed outside. It's not like farting under the blankets like some people."

Spencer ran his hand over his hair. "You ate Burger Boy, too?"

"That's beside the point," I cried. "There's a dead woman here, and you're focused on my gas."

"No, I'm not. I was talking about the molecules in the air, not your farts in the air."

He waved his hands around, like he was illustrating molecules flying through the air.

"You did something," he accused me. "First the chicken and the blood pressure machine, and now this. You did something to my peaceful town."

I crossed my arms in front of me and made a huffing noise, like I was offended, but I was really proud that he thought I had the ability to change molecules.

"I didn't do anything to your peaceful town. I didn't dress up like a chicken and rob the pharmacy. I didn't kill this poor woman."

Spencer snapped gloves on to his hands and crouched over the body. He muttered to himself something about peace and quiet and Crisco, but I wasn't paying close attention because there was another noise behind me, and this time I went into the orchard to investigate.

I heard a scuffling in the underbrush. It wasn't the sound of a bear, but something more human. Like humans. And they were laughing. No not laughing.

Giggling.

"Hey you! Stop!" I yelled and chased after the sound of people running ahead of me.

I might've been chasing after killers, and I had no idea what I would do if I caught them, but adrenaline filled my veins, and I couldn't stop myself if I tried.

And I didn't try.

"Stop!" I yelled again. I could hear them giggle, and I realized I was gaining on them.

Apple trees seemed to fly past me, as I ran. I wasn't an exerciser, and I was definitely not a runner, but I was experiencing a runner's high. Endorphins. Dopamine. I felt great. I felt omnipotent.

Wow, running was awesome. I took back

everything I had ever thought about people who wore knee socks and woke up at five to run around the block.

I was so rapturous about my ability to put one foot in front of the other, that it took me a moment to notice that the gigglers I was chasing had stopped and were blocking the path in front of me, facing me. I put on the brakes and skidded to a halt.

Ahead of me, two pre-teens stood their ground. They were wearing shorts and T-shirts.

And one of them was carrying a sheep.

They giggled, again.

My self-congratulatory attitude about my running ability made an about-face. I couldn't catch up to a kid carrying a sheep?

I looked closer. The sheep wasn't moving.

"Did you do something to that sheep?" I demanded.

They giggled, and the boy with the sheep threw it at me. I tried to dodge the sheep, but it hit me, and I fell to the ground with the sheep on top of me.

First the chicken, and now a sheep. I really had bad luck with farm animals.

But the sheep was much lighter then I would've thought, and I easily managed to get it off of me.

The boys had run off, and as far as I could tell, the sheep was dead. Or was it? I inspected it and found a large hole in its butt. And there was a *Made in China* stamp on its belly.

Oh, geez.

I lugged the fake sheep back to the scene of the crime. It only took a couple of minutes to walk there, and I realized that all of my patting on my back about my running ability had been totally exaggerated. I had run the equivalent of a half of a city block. When I arrived back at the scene of the crime, I tossed the fake sheep onto the ground. Remington had arrived, too, and he was holding his forensic kit in his hand.

"There you are," Spencer noted to me. "What did you get? Is that a sheep?"

"I think it's your victim's cousin."

"Is that a joke, Pinky?"

"Your murder victim," I said, pointing at the bloody woman. "Turn her over. I'll bet it'll be more obvious then."

"I don't think we should disturb the body like that," Remington said.

But Spencer had looked more closely at the sheep, and he was grinding his teeth.

"Turn it over," he ordered.

Remington and Brody turned her over. Sure enough, she had a red hole for a mouth and another red hole down below.

"Well, I'll be," Brody said.

Remington whistled low and long. "Plastics technology has come a long way. I thought it was a real woman."

"It's a sex doll," I announced. "I worked in a sex doll factory in Tulsa for two weeks once. But those were blowup dolls. Some of the guys brought in a helium tank once, and naked women were flying all over the factory. I still have nightmares from it. That was a weird job."

The three men stared at me without saying a word. I had had a long history of temporary jobs before I joined Grandma in her matchmaking business.

"You know what this means?" Spencer said.

"That we thought a sex doll was a murdered woman?" Remington guessed.

"No, it means that my peaceful town has returned. No murder. This was obviously a practical joke."

I nodded, sadly. "Yep. I saw the two kids. They thought they were very funny."

Spencer kissed me on the top of my head. "I'm sorry I accused you of changing the molecules. The blood pressure machine was just a slight aberration. All is well with the world."

After the sex doll and sex sheep were loaded in

Brody's trunk as evidence, Spencer drove me back to my car.

My client Susan Bass lived with her mother and grandmother in the same townhouse development as Bridget, outside of the Historic District. Her father and grandfather had died twenty years ago in a bizarre fishing accident. Since then, her mother and grandmother had doted on Susan like she was their lifeline. And maybe she was.

To them.

To me, she was a bridezilla.

Susan was my first wedding, and she had driven me crazy. I would've quit, but I had quit my life of quitting, and I was determined to see this through to the end. Besides, the entire town was invited, and I didn't want to fail in front of them. And Spencer would tease me. Since my idea of a fancy party was pigs-in-a-blanket and Netflix, he had made it clear about his doubts over my new business. I had to prove him wrong, no matter what.

I parked on the street, took a deep breath, and got out of my car. I slung my bag over my shoulder and remembered with dread that I hadn't washed my hair since the Crisco incident. So much for looking professional.

I plastered a smile on my face and thought happy

thoughts. Then, I walked up the walkway and rang the bell.

Susan's family's townhouse was identical to Bridget's. It had three floors, and the kitchen was on the second floor.

"There you are," Susan's mother greeted me. "Perfect timing. It's red alert over here. You need to fix it."

Oh, geez. I hoped the red alert wasn't about the caterer. If the caterer had backed out, I would have to cook, and I didn't think they wanted to serve toaster waffles at the wedding party.

"You bitch!" I heard Susan scream upstairs. "You bitch! You're ruining my wedding!"

"I'm sorry, Susan," I heard a girl squeak. "I didn't mean to... What're you doing? Put down the meat tenderizer. Susan, please put down the meat tenderizer!"

"It's been like this for an hour. You've got to fix it," Susan's mother told me.

I followed her upstairs. Susan's maid of honor, Tiffany, had her back to the refrigerator. Susan stood over her with a meat tenderizer clutched in her hand like a weapon.

"Help her," Susan's mother told me.

"Poor Tiffany. She's about to be tenderized," I said.

"No, not Tiffany. Help my daughter. All of this stress is going to wreck Susan's skin, and she'll look like a pepperoni pizza walking down the aisle on Saturday."

My stomach growled. Pepperoni pizza sounded good.

What was wrong with me? If I kept up this pace, they were going to have to cut a hole out of the wall for me to get out of Grandma's house.

I took a couple tentative steps forward, careful to stay out of Susan's reach.

"Now, now, what's all the fuss?" I asked in my sweetest wedding planner voice. I'd had to use that voice a lot lately with Susan. I had had a plan to crush up one of Lucy's Xanax into Susan's morning oatmeal, but Lucy had refused to give up any of her stash.

An unholy scream came out of Susan's mouth. "I'll tell you what the fuss is about," she screeched. I put my hands over my ears. She sounded like a cat in heat. "This bitch just got engaged."

"Neil asked your maid of honor to marry him?" I asked, honestly shocked.

Susan spun around and pointed the meat tenderizer at me. "Of course he didn't. How dare you suggest such a thing. Neil Chu loves me. Doesn't he love me? Why? What have you heard? Mom, Gladie said that Neil doesn't love me."

There was nothing like a wedding to make a woman have a psychotic break.

Braving the meat tenderizer, I gave Susan a big hug.

"Neil loves you," I told her in my sweet, calm voice, as I held her. "He's crazy about you. You're the Reese's peanut butter cup in his life. The Cap'n Crunch."

She sniffed. "He does love his Cap'n Crunch."

"So, tell me what happened."

"My bitch best friend got engaged. Four days before my wedding. Now my wedding's totally ruined."

She wiped her nose on my shirt. I had no idea how her friend's engagement ruined her wedding, but Susan also believed in the power of patent leather pumps, so I'd given up trying to make sense of her thinking long ago.

"Tiffany is... Is... Stealing my thunder," she cried and burst into rolling sobs onto my shoulder.

"I'm so sorry?" Tiffany said, like a question in her Valley Girl way of speaking. "I didn't mean to steal your thunder? I'm like the worst best friend in the world?" All of it was spoken like a question.

But Susan seemed to understand Tiffany's intentions. She let go of me and hugged her maid of honor.

"So, you'll cancel the engagement," she told her,

and it definitely didn't sound like a question.

"I can't do that. Johnny's parents are going to take us out to Applebee's. We can't cancel."

Susan did the cat scream, again.

It took three hours, but I convinced Susan that maids of honor only distracted from the beauty of the bride, and it would be much better to do without Tiffany under the lily-covered canopy and leave her in the front row instead, where she couldn't steal Susan's thunder.

Tiffany pouted a little about this decision to exclude her, but she wanted to wear her ring and go to Applebee's, so she finally relented.

After that crisis was averted, we discussed the details of the wedding party. I assured Susan that the axe-throwing room would be able to accommodate at least thirty people, and the tractor parade was good to go. I wasn't one hundred percent sure I could get the Longhorn bull to carry the couple to the party, though. That was proving to be a little difficult. But I decided not to worry Susan because I didn't want to be bludgeoned to death with a meat tenderizer.

When my stomach growled at five o'clock, I put an end to the meeting. Susan walked me to the door.

"You're not going to do that to your hair on my wedding day, are you?" Susan asked me with more than a touch of a threat in her voice.

My hand flew to my hair and withdrew it just as fast. It was still greasy. I'd forgotten about the Crisco.

"No, that was a one-time experiment," I assured her. "It won't happen again."

"Good. I don't know what you were thinking. I could squeeze out your hair and fry a batch of fries."

My stomach growled. Fries sounded good. I said goodbye and drove away in my Cutlass Supreme.

It was girls' night out with Lucy and Bridget. Normally, I would've stopped to pick up Bridget, but I was sure she would be teaching her toddler about the suffragette movement or labor rights, and I needed to rush home and de-Crisco myself before going out.

Driving into the Historic District, the neighborhood was even more quiet than usual. I opened my window and was hit with a dry wind that chapped my lips immediately. I turned left onto Cannes Boulevard, and was greeted by floodlights shining over the house across the street from mine.

I slowed down. Just ahead, there were construction trucks, a fire truck, and three police cars. Men stood around talking and standing nearby on the front lawn. Pablo stood with a big smile planted on his face.

And he was holding a skull.

GORED OF THE RINGS

CHAPTER 4

There will be times when your bride and groom will have shpilkes. You know what I mean. They want something new. Something exciting. And they'll get it, dolly! They will surely get it. But it might not be in the way they think they'll get it. They might look at something and not see it for the thing it really is. They might think: Feh, this thing is boring. This thing doesn't help my shpilkes. But if they give it time, they'll find out that they were wrong. The boring thing…that's what's going to get them going.

— Lesson 4, Wedding Business Advice From Your Grandma Zelda

I nearly crashed my car into the back of Remington's unmarked car, but I managed to brake in time.

Turning into my driveway, I saw Grandma standing with Meryl, watching the goings-on across the street. Pablo was still proudly holding the skull, and there was a lot of action and noise around him

"What's happening? Did Pablo kill someone?" I asked. "He's probably a serial killer."

"Hope springs eternal, huh, Gladie?" Meryl asked.

"They found the skull in the back when they were digging to enlarge the pool," Grandma explained.

My heart sank. "So, it's been there a long time." I thought of the house's last inhabitants. Could one of them have killed someone and built a pool over their grave? I wouldn't put it past them.

But Grandma seemed to read my mind. "The pool was built at the same time as the house in 1968, before the house was sold to the Terns. And the builder dropped dead from a perforated ulcer."

"Maybe one of the construction workers did it," Meryl suggested. "They're probably older than dirt now, though. I guess we could follow every old guy with a hammer in town and see if they killed someone and buried them under the pool."

What was going on? If there was a murder mystery, *I* was the one to solve it. Why wasn't anyone asking my opinion? Had the last three years of peace and quiet made everyone forget about my Miss Marple skills?

"Maybe I should go over there," I said meekly.

"Unless they're looking to fry up a chicken, I don't know what you could do," Meryl said, uncharitably. "They've even got an archaeology professor from San Diego over there. The skull has made quite a splash."

Grandma high-fived her friend. "Funny one, Meryl. Splash. Pool. Funny."

"You like that? I was quite the class clown in elementary school. I did a lot of tomfoolery."

Grandma smiled at Meryl. "I can see that in you. Tomfoolery."

Meryl was the blue-haired librarian, and she had spent at least fifty years spending her days shushing people and alphabetizing books. That didn't spell tomfoolery to me. But I was always bad in spelling, so what did I know.

"I think I left a scrunchie across the street," I lied and walked down the driveway.

The house across the street was a hive of activity. Meryl had been right. There was a lot of excitement about the skull. Excitement and worry. Five contractors were crossing themselves repeatedly. Spencer was talking to a couple of men, and I carefully sidestepped him and walked around to the back of Pablo's house without being detected.

The backyard was a mess. There was a small bulldozer on one side and a giant hole where the pool used to be. I carefully stepped around it, all the while looking down for clues.

I didn't know what I was looking for. Maybe more boxes. Maybe a confession note. But all I found were dirt and lizards.

I lost track of time, but at some point, I felt someone watching me, and I looked up to see Spencer eyeing me. His arms were crossed in front of him. Pablo was standing next to him. He was still holding the skull, and he looked pleased as punch.

"I was looking for my scrunchie," I lied.

Spencer arched an eyebrow. "What the hell is a scrunchie?"

"It's a woman's thing. You don't really want to know."

"Look at what the pool men found, Gladie," Pablo said. He took a few steps toward me with the skull in his outstretched arms like he was offering me a present. But he didn't let me touch it. He was like a kid who had just found the Golden Ticket, and he wasn't going to share.

"There's a big mucky-muck here from UCSD. He said this skull might belong to one of the town's original miners, or maybe a Comanche."

Spencer rolled his eyes. Everyone around Cannes knew that there had never been any Comanche in the area. Maybe the Iipay or the Kumeyaay.

"That's very exciting." I allowed.

Spencer smirked his little smirk. "Don't look so sad, Pinky. Archaeological finds are a good thing."

He was egging me on. A simple, academic, archaeological discovery fit in nicely with his craving for peace and quiet. And from his look, I knew that he knew that I was heartlessly wishing for a juicy murder.

"They didn't find any other bones, but I'm sure they're here," Pablo said, excited.

There was a noise, and from around the house came a long and elegant figure draped in peach organza. It was Lucy. She was perfectly put together as usual, and Bridget was by her side wearing big hoot owl glasses. She had applied a thick layer of blue eye shadow on her eyelids, and she was wearing a sandwich board over her clothes, which said *No to urban sprawl* on it in red letters.

"I got my causes confused," Bridget announced sadly, gesturing to her sandwich board. "I saw all of the trucks, and I was sure that they were digging up the Historic District to build condos."

"Look what was under my pool," Pablo told my friends with glee.

Lucy pointed at me. "Darlin', are you back to finding dead bodies? Phew. You sure did take some time off. I'm so glad you came back to yourself. So, whodunit?"

"Gladie didn't find the skull," Spencer told her. "The pool workers discovered it."

"It could be a Comanche or a miner," Pablo said.

"Oh drat, is that why I ruined my best pair of peach Jimmy Choos?" Lucy complained. "For a relic?"

"And I sandwich-boarded myself for nothing," Bridget complained.

I walked past Spencer and Pablo. I was disappointed, too. "Come on. I'm hungry," I told Lucy and Bridget.

Lucy drove Bridget and me to a fancy restaurant further up in the mountains. For years, we had eaten all of our meals at Saladz in the Historic District, but lately, we had started going out to dinner instead of lunch, and we were leaving the center of town to just get away. If I was bored with the peace and quiet, Bridget and Lucy were desperate to get away from their kids, even though they would never admit to that.

Bridget was deep in her plan to create an enlightened and feminist young man, who would work to right all of the wrongs of the world. And Lucy was trying to make her triplets into two Southern ladies and one Southern gentleman with the help of two nannies and a tutor.

All four children were in the same class at the local nursery school, and Lucy and Bridget were extremely active at the school.

Once we arrived at the restaurant, we were seated at a table by a window with an amazing view of the mountains and the orchards below us.

"Give me a Mint Julep, darlin'," Lucy told the waiter as soon as we were seated. I ordered a Diet Coke, and Bridget asked for pink lemonade. Lucy patted the table. "Listen ladies, we are not going to talk about children at this dinner. No sir. Tonight is a no-children zone."

Bridget nodded in agreement and pushed her glasses up on the bridge of her nose. "And we don't have to. There are so many other things to talk about. The dry weather has put a run on nose spray at the pharmacy, for example."

Our drinks arrived, and Lucy took a sip of her Mint Julep. "That's right. If I see one more person with their finger up their nose, I'm going to take off one of my Jimmy Choos and impale them with the spiky and flirtatious heel."

"The weather is very dry," I agreed.

"Booger weather. That's what Jonathan calls it,"

Bridget said of her toddler and then checked her phone. "I'm worried about him. His teacher said he's behind in scissor holding."

"Oh, darlin', you better get right on that. That sounds serious," Lucy said.

I didn't know scissor holding was a thing, and I certainly didn't know it was taught in school.

"And then there's the skull," I said, trying to steer them away from another kid conversation. Lucy knocked back the rest of her drink.

"Oh, the skull. Too bad it's archaeological, darling. I bet you'd love to sink your teeth into a juicy murder."

"Gladie doesn't need anyone to die to make her happy. She's in a healthy marriage, and she's starting a new business," Bridget said.

Lucy giggled. "Laura calls her do-do in the toilet her *business*," she said about one of her triplets. "She's so pretty in the dresses that I bought her, but she refuses to wear them."

"Jonathan calls her Spider-Man," Bridget said.

"I swear on Garth Brooks's head that I'm going to burn that Spider-Man costume, and then she'll have to wear Neiman Marcus and enjoy it!" Lucy exclaimed and ordered another Mint Julep.

The conversation moved on to nanny problems,

the preschool's cookie committee, and prickly heat. I ordered French fries and salmon and drifted off as I ate. I nodded occasionally so they would think that I was paying attention, but I was actually daydreaming about Pablo's backyard skull.

Did I need a murder to be happy? Was I happy? I was, but just like I loved French fries, I loved them more with ketchup.

By the time dinner was over, Lucy was blotto, so I drove her Mercedes back. I dropped Bridget off at her car in front of my house. Across the street, Pablo's house was quiet, and all of the workers had left.

Then, I drove Lucy home. Spencer was still there playing cards, and I knew that he could drive me home after I dropped off Lucy and her car.

Lucy lived up in the mountains in a gated community. When I parked in her large driveway, she turned to me and put her hand on my arm.

"I wish that skull was a juicy murder," she confessed.

"You do?"

"I love my children. You know I love my children, right, Gladie?"

"Of course. You built them a replica of Rodeo Drive in the backyard."

"Exactly. Only a mother who loves her children

would do that. But I'm tired of bedtime stories and bake sales. You know what I mean?"

I did. Lucy had gone from being a glamorous, cosmopolitan world traveler to being a glamorous suburbanite with three car seats in a minivan that she kept hidden in one of her garages.

"You just need a vacation," I suggested.

She leaned in close and spoke in a whisper. "We went to the Disney Resort in Hawaii for ten days. I almost beat Minnie Mouse to death with a pool noodle. They called in the police. I'm not allowed in any of the Disney properties anymore. Lifetime ban, Gladie. Lifetime. The nighttime nanny threatened to quit after that incident, but Harry doubled her salary for her to stay on. Don't tell the daytime nanny. She doesn't know."

"A lifetime ban sounds rough. But maybe you and Uncle Harry should go on a vacation without the kids."

Lucy recoiled in horror. "We couldn't do that. It would scar them. That's abandonment, Gladie."

"Sorry."

"But a murder. That only takes up half of a day here and there. That would get the blood pumping through my veins, again."

I felt her pain. I was anxious for some blood pumping, too.

An hour later, Spencer left with his winnings and drove us home in his car.

"It's still early," he said, driving down the winding road from the gated community. "We could go out for ice cream."

"Or we could have sex in the car by the lake."

The car swerved, and Spencer righted it. "Are you teasing me, Pinky?"

"There's a spot where we can park with a view of the lake, and it's a full moon. I get to be on top, and you'll have to push the seat back so the steering wheel doesn't bruise my ass."

Spencer made a sharp left in the direction of the lake. "I figure there's a seventy percent chance that I'm on *Candid Camera*, even though the show was canceled years ago. But I don't care. I'm not going to look a gift horse in the mouth."

"You're not calling me a horse, are you?"

"Not in your life. I don't want to put a wrench in the works."

"Nothing is going to put a wrench in these works. You're wearing my favorite suit, and your cologne is putting me over the edge. My lower half is humming. And throbbing."

He swerved the car, again, but got it back under control.

"I like when you say *throbbing*, Pinky. If you say you'll do that thing you do with my hair, I know I've died and gone to heaven."

"I'm going to do that thing with your hair," I assured him. "And all the other things, too."

"*All* the other things?"

"No, not *that* thing. It'll never be *that* thing."

CHAPTER 5

Beware what lies beneath, dolly! Doesn't that sound like a horror movie? Look at me, I'm Zelda Hitchcock. But seriously, beware the deep! You don't want some nebbish telling you one thing and then bam! something else is lying in wait for you. You get what I'm saying? Do your research. Ask all the questions. Look deep, bubbeleh.

— Lesson 5, Wedding Business Advice From Your Grandma Zelda

The next morning, Spencer and I made it downstairs an hour late. We had done all the things except the one thing in his car and then came home and did all the things except the one thing all over again in the shower. Then, we did a third round, the old-fashioned way in our bed.

I could barely walk.

Spencer looked a little saddle worn, too. But he was extremely grateful and kept kissing my head.

"Thank you," he said. "Thank you. Thank you. Thank you. I don't know what I did to deserve you. Maybe I was Gandhi in a previous life."

"Gandhi had nothing to do with it," I said and grabbed his ass.

His eyes grew dark, and he pulled me in close to him. "I could call in sick. Lovesick. We could spend the day just kissing, if you want."

To further tempt me, he gave me a sampling of his kissing talents. He had oodles of kissing talents. Spencer was an amazingly talented kisser. His tongue explored my mouth, making me dizzy. My eyes rolled back in my head, and I moaned. He pulled me closer, and I could feel that he was ready to go.

But then reality crept its ugly face in my mind, and I broke off the kiss.

"I have to lock down the bull today, or my bride is going to meat tenderize me," I told him.

Spencer blinked. "Is that sex talk? Are you talking dirty to me?"

"No."

"Because if you are, that's fine. I'll go along with it. Let me tenderize you, baby."

I stepped out of his embrace. "I'm not talking dirty to you. My client wants to ride a bull from her ceremony to her party."

"Weddings are stupid," he growled.

I didn't take his comment personally. He was still upset that our wedding was to blame for the destruction of our dream house across the street.

Since Grandma had already eaten breakfast and was busy consoling a match over his breakup, Spencer and I decided to go to Tea Time together.

I ordered a latte and cranberry scone, and Spencer ordered a double espresso and two apple turnovers.

The calories and caffeine were welcome. Twelve hours of sex could really take it out of a girl. I knew that I had been trying to fill a void with Spencer's penis and overturn melancholy with orgasms, but sex with Spencer was amazing, no matter if I had used it as a drug.

"Holy smokes, you two have no shame," Ruth sneered at us when we sat in the center of the tea shop. She stood over our table with her hands on her hips, looking down her nose at us.

"We weren't picking our noses, Ruth," Spencer insisted.

"Not that, although if I see one more customer with his finger up his nose, I'm going to cut it off. What's with these people? Why are they so freaked out about a little dry weather? If they love humidity so much, they should move to Florida. It's cheaper there."

She harrumphed and took a deep breath, like she was preparing to complain for a lot longer. "Dry heat is good for a body," she continued. "Look at me. My bones should be dust by now, but I'm still going strong. I had to move fifty-pound bags of coffee this morning. You don't see those ancient Floridians doing that. No sirree. And my joints haven't seen cartilage since Carter was president, but you don't hear me complaining."

"That's true," Spencer said with his mouth full. "You're famous for never complaining."

Ruth narrowed her eyes at him. "You better not be sarcastic there, cop. Anyway, you two smell like sex."

"But we showered, Ruth," I said, embarrassed.

We also had had sex in the shower. Maybe we needed to get a stronger body wash.

"Look at you," she continued, loudly. "Face is flushed. Hair all over the place. Droopy eyelids. It's either sex or malaria."

Everyone in the tea shop turned to look at us, probably to determine whether we had just had sex or not. My face grew hot, and I was sure that I looked like an eggplant.

"Did you hear about your neighbor?" Ruth asked me, moving on from the topic of my sex life.

"What? Does the Museum of Natural History want the skull he found?" I asked. I was still peeved about the skull.

"How would I know? What I do know is that Pablo's workers have walked off the job. They said the house is cursed and the skull is the work of the devil. Pablo's pool has been canceled, along with his indoor Jacuzzi."

Spencer looked up from his turnover. "Indoor Jacuzzi. Damn, I always wanted an indoor Jacuzzi. Maybe I could fix our bathtub, turn it into a Jacuzzi."

Oh, geez. If Spencer "fixed" the bathtub, I would never get to take a bath again.

"Pablo's got a lot of money, you know," Ruth continued. "He paid in cash. But those workers won't return for anything. He even tried to pick up the workers from next door at the mystery store, but the word already got around about the curse and the devil."

Spencer wiped his mouth with a napkin. "You should never tell a cop that someone's paying in cash. It sets off law enforcement bells."

As if on cue, his phone rang, and he answered. "Murder? Are you sure?" he asked into the phone after a minute. "How's that possible? He did what? What the hell? I'll be right there." He stood and put his phone in his pocket. "No," he told me.

"No what?"

"No, you're not coming with me. You have bulls and tenderizing to deal with."

He was totally right. My priorities had to be with the first wedding I was handling. My whole business was counting on it. I couldn't afford to fail. Without a bull, Susan would be livid. And a livid bride meant that I would be out of the wedding business before I was ever really in it.

"You're totally wrong," I lied. "I have plenty of time to lock down the bull. More than enough time to take a detour at a murder scene."

Spencer shook his head, like he would brook no discussion. "No."

"Save yourself a lot of trouble and even more energy, cop," Ruth told him. "She's going to get there one way or another. This way you can keep an eye on her."

Spencer sighed. "Fine. And it's not a murder scene. It's an almost-murder scene."

It was an almost-murder scene. At least that's what Farmer Joe told us. It took a long time to get the details out of him because he was completely hysterical.

"That bitch!" he yelled. He yelled that word a lot.

We were up high in the mountains. So high that

we could see the orchards below us. Farmer Joe had a cranberry bog, something I didn't know even existed in Southern California.

The bog was enormous, like a small lake, and it was filled with floating cranberries. It reminded me of Thanksgiving and the turkey and cranberry sandwiches I loved to eat during the week after the holiday.

What was wrong with me lately? I couldn't stop eating.

Remington was standing next to a middle-aged woman with curly black hair and a satisfied smile planted on her face.

It didn't take a detective or a psychic to determine that she was the bitch. Farmer Joe kept pointing at her and calling her that.

"Where's the dead body?" I asked him.

"Me!" he shouted, pounding his chest with the palms of his hands, like he was Tarzan. "I'm the dead body. At least I was going to be the dead body if the bitch had had her way!"

"His wife," Remington explained to me, gesturing at the woman, like she was a prize on the *Price is Right*.

Farmer Joe was soaking wet, and there were cranberries lodged in his hair and his ears. He was wild-eyed, both terrified and angry as spit at the same time.

I sighed and looked at the time on my phone. The morning was ticking away. It was Wednesday, and I had a million things to do before Saturday's wedding. And here I was in the middle of nowhere with no dead body, only a man accusing his wife of being a bitch.

I gnawed on the inside of my cheek and was hit with a sudden craving for Pop-Tarts

"What is your exact complaint, sir?" Spencer asked Farmer Joe.

"That bitch put something in the bog to eat me."

"Your wife wanted to eat you?"

"No not my wife," Farmer Joe said, sounding exhausted and beside himself with frustration. "She wanted *the thing* to eat me."

"Great movie, *The Thing*," Remington said. "Both versions."

Remington was a buff, hotter than hell detective and part-time MMA fighter, but he was also a number one, Grade A geek. Last month, he dressed up as baby Yoda at Comic-Con. He had shown me the photos.

Spencer ran a hand over his hair. "Let me get this straight. Your wife put a thing in the bog to eat you. What kind of thing?"

Farmer Joe put his hands out as wide as he could stretch them. "A big thing. A creature from the deep."

"*The Creature from the Black Lagoon*," Remington

announced. "Another great flick."

"Was that what she put in the bog?" Spencer asked Farmer Joe. "A monster?"

Farmer Joe shook his head. "Not a monster. A creature. A prehistoric creature that came up from the depths of the bog and nearly killed me."

He turned around and showed us his back. Sure enough, the back of his shirt had been ripped to shreds.

Spencer scowled at me. I knew that scowl. It was the same scowl that he used when he accused me of creating a chicken burglar out of thin air. And now he was probably blaming me in his head about a crazy man and his fear that a prehistoric creature was hunting him in his bog.

"If you want, I'll sign off on a seventy-two-hour psychiatric hold for him," Farmer Joe's bitch wife offered.

Farmer Joe put his hand out, palm forward. "I swear to God that there is a creature in that water, and that bitch put it in there. She warned me last night that she was going to watch me die in the bog, and today, when I was swimming for my life away from the prehistoric creature, I saw her standing on the shore smiling at me."

We all looked at his wife, who was still smiling with smug satisfaction. Then, we all turned to the bog. We stood silent for a long while, as we watched the quiet bog for a creature.

The water was still with only slight movement by the floating cranberries. Then, suddenly there was a splashing noise from across the bog, and I saw a long, scaly back slice through the water at a fast clip.

"Holy crap, it's a Loch Ness Monster," I breathed.

"See? See?" Farmer Joe said, jumping up and down in excitement. "She put the creature in there to kill me."

"This is just like the Elvira horror movie night from back in the day," Remington said. "This whole thing should be in black-and-white, and Vincent Price should be narrating it."

"Keep it together, bro," Spencer told his detective. "There's got to be a reasonable explanation. Ma'am, did you put something in the bog?"

The woman shrugged and kept smiling. She was starting to creep me out, and I believed what Farmer Joe said about her.

Spencer stepped to the edge of the bog and looked down into it. "It was probably a trick of the eye, just like the Loch Ness Monster."

Suddenly, a huge prehistoric creature leapt from the water. Its large jaws were open, and it lunged at Spencer's head with amazing precision. It was going to eat my husband's head. It was going to bite it clean off.

I don't know what came over me. I was imbued with superhuman powers, probably because I was afraid that my future orgasms were in danger, or maybe I just loved Spencer and didn't want him hurt.

Whatever the reason for my surge of lightning-fast reflexes and Incredible Hulk strength, I flew through the air and miraculously made it to Spencer before the prehistoric creature did.

I tackled my husband just in time and rolled him to the side, just as the creature's jaws snapped closed with a loud noise and its body landed on the ground where Spencer had been standing.

"You attacked me, Pinky," Spencer said, clearly shocked. His lip was bleeding, and one of his eyes look like it was going to turn black and blue.

"I saved you from the prehistoric creature. I'm the hero in your story," I told him.

"Get out of the way!" Remington shouted.

Spencer and I scrambled to safety, as the creature ran away on short, stubby legs.

Remington sighed. "That was disappointing. It was only an alligator."

It was an alligator. A huge, monstrous alligator that almost killed Spencer.

"Are there alligators in California?" Spencer

asked, as we watched the alligator slink off into the forest

"I saw a couple in the San Diego zoo. Maybe one escaped," I suggested.

"The bitch works concessions at the San Diego Zoo!" Farmer Joe announced and pointed at his wife.

"Holy crap, she stole an alligator," I said. "That's ruthless."

"That alligator must be at least fifteen feet long. How did you get it here?" Remington asked.

"Little-known fact," she told him. "Alligators will do anything for apple pie."

"Holy shit," Spencer breathed.

Cannes was known for its apple pie. People came to Cannes from all around for a slice of our famous apple pie. We had so many pie shops in the Historic District that the entire neighborhood smelled of hot apple pie at all times of the day and night.

Dammit, now I wanted apple pie.

"Did you hear that, Chief? The town is in danger," Remington said.

"It's a good ten miles into town," Spencer pointed out. "It's an alligator. He can't go that far."

"It's seven miles," Remington corrected him.

"It did go in the direction of town," I pointed out.

Spencer stomped his foot on the ground. "This is

just perfect. Perfect! There's a giant alligator let loose on the town. A giant alligator came out of the bog, and now it's going to terrorize the town for its apple pie. That means that I have to hunt a giant alligator. I have to hunt a giant alligator in an Armani suit."

"The alligator wasn't wearing an Armani suit," Farmer Joe said. "Oh, you mean you're wearing an Armani suit. Got it."

"You don't look so good," I told Spencer. "Your eyes are rolling around."

"They're my alligator hunting eyes, Pinky. You've never seen them before."

Remington arrested Farmer Joe's wife for attempted murder and theft of a wild animal. Spencer went into the woods to capture the alligator with a piece of rope he found in the trunk of his car. It turned out the alligator was an endangered species and had to be captured alive, but the San Diego Zoo refused to help because of budget cuts.

Fred picked me up and drove me home. I ran inside the house to pee before I had to go secure the bull, but Grandma stopped me and handed me a scrap of paper.

"I found it on the door," she explained. "It's from Pablo. He wants to talk to Spencer. He must've come over when I was in back, gardening."

"I'll let Spencer know, but I think he's going to be busy for a while chasing an alligator."

"Poor Spencer. That's not going to end well."

"Don't I know it."

CHAPTER 6

When in doubt, add flowers. Isn't that the truth for everything in life? I sometimes think that if only that mamzer Stalin had just had a nice vase of fresh-cut flowers on his desk, he wouldn't have been so grumpy and wouldn't have killed so many people. He would have been content to smell the flowers. And that's the way it is with your bride and groom. Her dress is wrinkled. His breath stinks. But who cares? All they see are the flowers because they look nice and they smell nice. It's not a bubbe-meise to believe that one's surroundings affect a mood. That goes double for a wedding. I mean, look at that meshuganah Virginia Woolfe. She was crazy about a room of her own. Maybe she was so crazy about it that it made her kill herself? Who knows. Just add the flowers.

— Lesson 6, Wedding Business Advice From

GORED OF THE RINGS

Your Grandma Zelda

I rang Susan's doorbell at six a.m. I was armed with a large suitcase filled with emergency supplies and six lattes from Tea Time.

Susan's mother opened the door. Her hair was up in curlers, and one eye was bordered with a fake eyelash, making it look like she was winking at me.

"You're already doing your hair and makeup?" I asked. "I have people coming for that."

My hairdresser Bird was going to do the hair, and she had a makeup person who she said could turn Dick Cheney into Angelina Jolie. They were set to come at nine o'clock, two hours before the ceremony.

"Susan was afraid that they wouldn't show up in time, so we started ourselves."

A tear popped out of her eye and rolled down her cheek, taking the fake eyelash with it. A chill of foreboding went up my spine.

"How bad is it?" I asked.

"Two hours ago, Susan decided that she needed to go with curls instead of a sleek updo with tendrils."

Her voice cracked in the middle, and she started to cry in earnest. Her tears pushed her eyelash under her runny nose, and now she looked like Hitler.

I felt the pressure of a wave of hysterical giggles

build inside me, and I clamped my teeth over the inside of my cheek to hold them back.

Then, her words hit me. "Curly? How curly?" I asked.

"Curly. Like the eighties curly."

"She didn't."

She snapped. Her Hitler mustache danced around as she blubbered. "She did. Home permanent. She found an old box in my medicine cabinet, and she went to town."

A home permanent? It was the worst news possible.

"How bad is it?"

"She left it on too long. That was my fault. I need new readers. My eyesight is slipping, and I read the time wrong. She left it on for twice the suggested time."

I closed my eyes. Why did I want to go into business on my own? Matchmaking with my grandmother had been going so well.

"So how bad is it?" I asked.

"She's bald on one side, and the other side looks like she's Ethel Rosenberg after the electric chair."

"I don't hear her. I would've thought I could hear her," I noted. I should have heard her in the act of killing someone or setting fire to the house, at the very least. I was more than a little surprised that Susan had let her mother live.

Susan's mother leaned forward and lowered her voice so I could barely hear her. "That's the spooky thing, Gladie. She hasn't said a word since she saw herself in the mirror. She's sitting upstairs on the toilet with a handful of her hair clenched in her hand. She hasn't uttered a sound. She hasn't blinked, either."

I took my phone out of my purse and called Bird. "Red alert. Red alert," I cried into the phone. "All hands on deck. I repeat, all hands on deck. Send in reinforcements. This is a code red, pandemic, nuclear holocaust, level one emergency."

"Oh, my God. Say it isn't so," she said into the phone. "Not a home permanent. Anything but that."

Wedding planning is a terrifying business. For many people, their wedding day is the most important day of their life. A day that they'll remember forever.

So, the weight on the wedding planner's shoulders is immense. The burden, almost unbearable. Luckily, a smart wedding planner has a team around her to help carry the burden. I had Bird, who was stone-cold competent under pressure. Not only was she a whiz-bang hairstylist, but she was also a general, in charge of her troops with a kind, yet firm hand.

I also had an awesome caterer. Debbie Porter had

recently gotten divorced, and I had asked her to start her own business because, just as I knew that it was going to be eighty-five-degrees today with three percent humidity, I knew that Debbie would succeed beyond her wildest dreams as a caterer. So far, she had, but this would be the first time she was working with me.

The wedding ceremony was going to be held in the small Catholic church in town, and the party was going to be outside at the winery near the lake. Debbie had hired an army of servers to help with the buffet lunch and appetizers.

While Bird worked on Susan's hair, I called Debbie to make sure everything was on target.

"I got it all under control!" she yelled into the phone. There was a deafening sound where she was that she had to shout over. "They're revving up the tractors for the parade! The axe room tent is almost done!"

"Almost?" I asked, panicked. "They were supposed to set up last night."

"There was a mishap, but they sewed his finger back on."

"Who? Who? Whose finger?"

"I don't know. He has a handlebar mustache and a face tattoo of a hand flipping the bird. Hey, that's ironic. He cut his middle finger off."

There was a loud crash in the background.

"What was that?" I asked.

"An idiot who doesn't know how to drive a tractor."

It was time to put out the fires. I would have preferred for someone else to put out the fires, but I was in charge. I was the fireman. I hung up with Debbie.

"I'm going to have to go, but I'll be back by nine o'clock," I told Bird.

She had brought over the entire staff from her salon and had been going at it hard on Susan for an hour.

"How is she doing?" I asked Bird.

"I saw her blink fifteen minutes ago. That's an improvement. We've got the beauty thing handled. Someone should call the Nobel committee for this one. I'm an artist and a scientist. Both at the same time."

I gave her a quick hug. "Thank you. I'll be back in a hurry."

I took my fourth latte with me and drove like a bat out of hell to the wedding party area. I had already double-checked the church at four in the morning, and everything there was perfect and ready to go.

I heard the venue before I saw it. It was the sound of tractors revving their engines. Even though Neil was a biotechnician from San Diego, he was a big Western fan, and it was his idea for the tractor parade and Longhorn bull ride to the party. Susan had had the idea for the axe-throwing room.

I found Neil revving a tractor while he was wearing a tux. His three groomsmen were also revving tractors, and one tractor was idling on its side against the tree.

"Turn it off!" I shouted over the noise.

Neil turned his head toward me, and I screamed in horror and took three steps backward.

"Your face! Your face!" I cried. It was so much worse than a home permanent. His mouth was swollen. Not just swollen. Grotesquely swollen. His lips were huge, and his tongue was sticking out, and it was the size of a large salami.

"I bot bibin," he said.

"What?"

His groomsmen exploded into hysterics, doubled over and slapping their thighs with laughter. They dropped down from the tractors.

"A rattlesnake bit his tongue," one of them told me and broke into hysterics again.

I checked the ground and hopped up and down. "Here? There are rattlesnakes here? You need to get to a hospital."

It turned out that Neil had actually spent the night in the hospital and left early to make it to the wedding on time. But he shouldn't have been out of the hospital. He looked like he was on his way to being dead in a hurry.

"Wait a minute," I said, interrupting their recounting of the hospital trip. "How did a rattlesnake bite his tongue?"

"Bacher pahpee," Neil told me.

"Bachelor party? Bachelor party?" My voice rose, and I sounded like a very angry Glinda Good Witch of the North. I shook my finger at the groomsmen. "What kind of bachelor party was that?" I demanded.

The groomsmen high-fived Neil. "The best!" one of them yelled.

"Totally off the chain," another said.

They spoke with thick Texas accents, even though they worked with Neil in San Diego, and I knew for a fact that they had all grown up together in Irvine. Somewhere along the line, they had all picked up a love of Texas, tractors, and axes, and I was paying the price for it.

"Shouldn't he take some Benadryl?" I asked, concerned. He looked like he had a red balloon attached to his face. I didn't know how he could breathe.

He put his finger against his right butt cheek. "Bot eh ass," he told me. "Bot eh ass."

"Shot in ass?" I asked.

"The hospital shot him up, man," one of the

groomsmen told me.

I put two fingers against the side of my neck and felt for my pulse. It was like a hummingbird's, faint and going a mile a minute. That was good. It might have meant that I was going to have a heart attack and die before the wedding. That would be a relief.

"Get these tractors in line!" I shouted, suddenly. "I want to see a nice tight formation, and get them over to Susan's place on the double. Remember, you're parading her to the church. You're not going to mess this up for me. Do you hear me?"

They heard me. I used the voice that Lucy used with her cleaning ladies when they forgot to clean behind the curtains. And it worked.

Neil and his groomsmen got control of the tractors and started to drive them away.

I called ahead to Bird and warned her that Susan's groom looked like his face had exploded. Bird told me that Susan's hair and makeup were done, and that she was coming out of her catatonic state. She also promised to crush Ativan into Susan's orange juice to ward off hysteria when she finally saw Neil and his swollen tongue.

I ended the call. Phew. At least those two crises were averted. I still had some time before I had to get back to Susan, so I decided to inspect the party grounds and make sure everything was going to plan. I found

Debbie giving instructions to her waiters. She was extremely professional, and I immediately felt better about the wedding's chances for success.

"If in doubt, follow Colin's lead," she told the waiters, gesturing at a middle-aged man with a thick head of salt-and-pepper hair, dressed in the same uniform as everyone else. "Colin knows the drill."

"How about the axe? Does Colin know axe?" one of the waiters called out, and everyone snickered.

"Shut up, Matt," Debbie said. "First rule of catering is don't make fun of the customers."

She winked at me, and I winked back. Half of the tables have been set up, and there were two tents. One was for dancing, and the other was for axe throwing.

I went into the dancing tent. Susan had wanted the tables outside but the dance floor and band in a tent, presumably to separate the generations. The dance floor was already in place, and the bandstand was nearly complete. I waved to the florist, who was starting on the tent after finishing at the church.

The axe-throwing tent didn't look as bad as I thought it would. The florist had already decorated, and someone had thoughtfully put a rug over the bloodstain where the axe worker had cut off his finger. A series of axes were hung on a mobile wall, and on the other side of the tent, there were four large targets, which were backed with hay.

A flash of dread passed through my body, and I braced myself for one of my now-familiar visions, but there was nothing. Only dread.

"Strange," I said out loud.

I squeezed my eyes shut and tried to fire up my third eye.

It worked. I saw a hot, dry day. I saw Matt the caterer picking his nose as he served champagne. I saw Neil's tongue return to normal during the second dance. I saw Spencer look dashing in his suit. And I saw that Pablo was hiding something. No, I *knew* he was hiding something.

I opened my eyes.

What was Pablo hiding? Was that what was provoking the feeling of dread? I had no clue. I couldn't see anything else. My third eye was letting me down.

My phone rang. "Come quick," Bird said on the line. "Susan saw her nails. She wanted passion pink, but we only have cotton candy pink."

"Oh my God," I breathed. "I'll be right over."

Spencer wrapped an arm around my waist and pulled me close to his side. "Looks like you're a hit. I take back everything I thought about your wedding business," he told me and kissed the side of my neck.

I looked around me. The ceremony had gone off without a hitch. Even the tractor parade had been flawless. Susan hadn't seemed to notice that her groom's tongue was larger than his forehead. The food was delicious, and even Matt the waiter was acting professionally.

There had been a tiny incident with the Longhorn bull, which carried the newly married couple to the party, when it decided to drive its horn into a Mini Cooper's back tire. But otherwise, all was well. The bull was tied up behind the axe throwing tent, which much to my surprise, was a big hit.

"You're forgiven," I told Spencer. "I don't blame you for thinking those thoughts. I thought it was all over when I saw Neil's tongue."

Grandma was sitting at a table with Ruth and I left Spencer to say hello. Grandma had matched Neil and Susan, and Ruth was her plus-one at the wedding.

"The waiter picked his nose while he served me champagne," Ruth complained to me.

"Maybe you can get back at him in the axe-throwing tent," I suggested.

"That's the first sensible thing you've ever said to me, girl," Ruth told me.

Out of the corner of my eye, I saw Pablo talking with Susan. He was obviously inebriated, and he was practically slobbering all over her. He kept invading her personal space, and she retreated until she had backed up against the table. I trotted over there to diffuse the situation before it got out of hand.

"Come on, baby. Someone who looks as hot as you shouldn't be so angry. It'll give you frown lines," he was telling her as I got near.

Susan poked him in the chest, hard. "Listen, pal. I'm not paying for your stupid painting."

"How are we all doing?" I interrupted in my sweet, wedding planner voice. "I hear everyone's raving about the shrimp puffs, and Bridget has had four mini crab cakes and she said they're the best ever."

"You will pay for the painting, one way or another," Pablo told Susan and leered at her, ignoring me.

"I will not. My cousin Leo could have done a better job, and he's seven years old."

Pablo turned to me. "They wanted a painting of her and her husband riding a tiger. Of course, it looked like a child's painting."

"Tigers are beautiful," Susan said in my direction.

I caught Spencer's eye, urging him to come over with a look. He understood the situation immediately and reached us in a couple strides.

He slapped Pablo's back. "Hey there, man.

How's it going?" he asked jovially.

Quickly, I steered Susan away. "We're not going to pay for that painting," she told me adamantly, when we were out of Pablo's earshot. "Anyway, it's a fortune. Much more than we thought it would be. There is no way we're paying for it. If we do, how will we afford our dining room set?" I steered her toward Grandma, who knew how to calm down anyone. "Gladie, Pablo threatened to sue us. I'll kill him if he does that," Susan told me.

I left her with my grandmother when I saw one of the groomsmen, Brian Bishop, storm over to Pablo and Spencer.

"You!" Brian yelled at him. "Hands off my boy's girl!"

I skipped toward them. "Can't we all be friends?" I sing-songed in my wedding planner voice.

"I'm going to kill you," Brian growled at Pablo.

Spencer put a hand on Brian's chest and pushed him back, slightly. "Don't be an idiot. You don't threaten a man in front of a cop. What a moron."

Brian blinked and stepped away in a hurry.

"Does everyone at this wedding want you dead?" I asked Pablo. It was a harsh thing to say, but I was worried that all of the animosity toward Pablo was going to tarnish my wedding victory.

"Only the ones who owe me money," Pablo answered. I followed his gaze toward Debbie. I couldn't imagine why she would have owed him money.

"I saw your note that you wanted to talk to me, but I've been busy hunting an alligator," Spencer told Pablo. "What can I do for you?"

Smooth. Spencer knew how to talk to people. He was a social worker with a gun. His skillset came in handy.

Something flashed over Pablo's face, and I realized it was the thing he was hiding, but I still didn't know what it was.

"Oh, that," he said and waved Colin the waiter over. "That was nothing. I don't need to talk to anyone."

Colin presented Pablo with a tray of mini crab cakes, and Pablo took one.

"Anything wrong?" Spencer asked Pablo. "You can tell me anything. We can go somewhere more private if you want to talk."

Pablo shook his head. "No, I've never been happier. I don't have a problem in the world. On the contrary."

Colin turned away, but Pablo grabbed him by the collar and pulled him back. "I wasn't done," Pablo exclaimed. "I wanted another crab cake."

Colin whipped around, and the tray flew into the

air and landed on his head. He turned bright red. He was the model of professionalism, and he was not taking the slight failure in stride.

"You know what?" I said to Pablo. "You haven't seen the axe-throwing tent."

Grabbing hold of Pablo's hand, I tugged him toward the tent. The wedding had been going so well, but my famous artist neighbor, who had always been very amiable, turned out to be a toxic presence. It was probably nothing more than too much champagne on only a handful of finger foods, but if I wanted the wedding party to end without incident, I needed to distract him.

Inside the tent, the action was definitely distracting. Folks were having a lot of fun, throwing axes at the targets. Unfortunately, the tent was filled with Susan, Brian, and Debbie. Everyone who hated Pablo or at least owed him money. The only one who didn't want to kill him was Lucy and the man in charge of the axes.

I steered Pablo toward Lucy.

"Check this out, darlin'," Lucy told me. "I'm holding an axe. I'm Paul Bunyan in a Stella McCartney original."

There was a loud noise from just outside the tent, and the tent pole shook a little.

"It sounds like someone's giving birth," Lucy

noted.

"Oh, no, it's the bull," I said. By now, I was familiar with its sounds. I had seen its handler sitting at one of the tables, and that meant the bull was alone and unattended.

I asked the axe monitor for help, and we left together to see what was happening with the longhorn bull. On our way out of the tent, Colin was walking in. He had found another platter of mini crab cakes and was offering it to the tent's inhabitants.

Great. Now, everyone who hated Pablo was in a small, enclosed space with him. I hoped Lucy could keep him distracted. The axe guy and I walked out and around to the back of the tent.

"I will not stop killin' you, artist man!" I heard Lucy yell.

Fabulous. Now Lucy hated him, too. Pablo was an aggression magnet.

Around the outside of the tent, we found the bull. It had gotten tangled in the leather strap that tied it to the tent. It struggled against it to get free, and the whole tent moved with it.

"Do something," I told the axe guy.

"What? You want me to throw an axe at the bull? It's an easy target. I could do it, if you want."

"No, maybe you can just hold on to it."

He looked at me like I had sprouted a second head. "The bull must weigh two tons, and its horns are three feet long. I was kicked out of school in tenth grade, but I ain't stupid."

"Fine, I'll do it," I said, annoyed.

I approached the animal gingerly, talking to it the entire time. But it must not have found my sweet wedding planner voice comforting because it bucked and reared. Its eyes were wide, and it looked around, as if it was trying to figure out a way to escape my pursuit.

"Calm down. I won't hurt you," I told the enormous animal.

The bull made a horrible noise and lunged at me. I sidestepped it and rolled to the side on the ground, just as I had done with the alligator.

And just like with the alligator, the bull kept going. He put his head down and speared the axe-throwing tent with its deadly horns. There were screams from inside the tent as it fell like a house of cards. The screams continued as the tent smothered them, and the bull managed to free itself and then ran across the vineyard, trampling the grapes. His handler ran after him.

"My wife's in there!" Neil yelled.

He hopped onto one of the tractors, and he and his groomsmen pulled the tent off of the trapped people inside.

"Is everyone all right?" I called in my wedding planner voice and began to count heads.

Susan, Brian, Debbie, Colin, and Lucy were all fine. Colin had dropped another platter, and Susan's hairdo had gotten destroyed, revealing her home permanent. But otherwise, everyone was okay.

"Wait a minute," I said, remembering. "Where's Pablo?"

"He must have run away," Lucy said. "The lecherous coward. He pinched my behind. I wanted to kill him."

The feeling of dread went up my spine, again. "We have to find him," I said with urgency. "We have to find him, *now.*"

It didn't take long. A minute later, Brian found him.

Pablo Cohen was lying under the fallen wall of axes.

And he had an axe embedded through his face, perfectly placed right down the middle.

Susan screamed and threw up all over Brian. Debbie fainted, and Colin started to hyperventilate and whimper.

"Will you look at that?" Lucy said. "What're the odds?"

CHAPTER 7

Spice is the spice of life. Did you see what I did there, bubbeleh? I was clever with my words. You might ask: which spice is the spice of life? And I would answer: All of them! Just make sure your life is spicy. That includes weddings. So, if your bride wants a hot pink dress with a glitter-covered tube top, let her do it. It's spicy. Sure, she might kvetch later, but give her what she wants. When things get spicy, they get interesting, and nobody wants a boring wedding.

– Lesson 7, Wedding Business Advice From Your Grandma Zelda

"I think he's dead," Neil said.

"You think?" Ruth asked him. "You must be a card-carrying MENSA member. The man has an axe through his face. See that pink stuff squishing out? That's his brain, Einstein. And for your information, brains don't do that when, you know, a person is alive."

Boy, ever since Ruth had gotten off her hormone replacement, she had gone up a notch in snark.

"I don't feel very well," Grandma said. She had turned a light shade of green. Weirdly, I felt fine. Not hungry, but not sick to my stomach at all.

"I'll take you home, Zelda," Ruth offered. "I've seen enough, too."

The entire wedding party had seen enough. They had all formed a circle around poor Pablo's axed body. Two guests had taken photos before Spencer read them the riot act and made them stop.

"What a terrible accident," Lucy said. "A crazy one, like fate has perfect aim."

"I can't believe he's dead," Debbie said.

Susan's mother stomped over to me and waved her finger under my nose. "If you think I'm going to pay you after this, you're crazy. And I'm calling my cousin Maury. He's a lawyer, and he's going to sue you. I hope you have insurance."

"Uh…" I said.

An ambulance drove onto the lawn by the tent, and that seemed to signal that the party was over. Susan and her mother put the rest of the cake in the back of her Camry, and Susan hurled her bouquet at Tiffany with a hard, overhand toss.

The groomsmen filtered out, and then it was only Spencer, a few cops, the paramedics, Debbie and her staff, Pablo, and I left.

I stepped closer and studied Pablo. The wall of axes had toppled over on him, but now it was lying on its side. Presumably, the bull had knocked it over, and an axe had dislodged from the wall, finding Pablo's face with amazing precision and force. The axe was deep in Pablo's face. It was a hell of a shot *if* it had really been an accident.

"Pinky, you're going to need to leave the area," Spencer told me. "The coroner needs to do his work. I'm so sorry about this accident. I hope it doesn't hurt your business. Truly."

He kissed me lightly on the lips, and I walked away. Debbie and her staff were cleaning up in a hurry. I imagined that they wanted to get as far away from Pablo's dead body as they could and as quickly as possible.

I found Colin stacking trays in the back of Debbie's catering van.

"What happened in there?" I asked him.

"That's what the police wanted to know, but I can't be much help, unfortunately," he said, taking a minute to sit on the van's bumper. "The tent came down, and it all went dark."

"Did anything happen with Pablo before then?

Right before? Did he argue with someone, for example?"

"Not that I noticed."

"Was he talking to someone? Was he standing with someone?"

Colin seemed to think about that for a second. "There was the Southern woman. He was with her."

My heart sank. "Yes," I said, thanked him, and went to my car.

Spencer was working late. With an alligator on the loose and a local dead in a freak accident, he had hours of paperwork to complete and about a hundred witnesses to interview.

I had come home and took a long, hot bath. Then, Grandma and I ate whitefish salad on toasted rye bread with barbecue potato chips. After, I went up to the attic to my office.

I cleared off a space on my desk and laid out five notecards. I wrote a name on each card: Susan Chu, Brian Bishop, Debbie Porter, Colin Bacon, and Lucy Smythe.

I didn't want to write on the last card, and when I saw Lucy's name printed in my handwriting, I wanted to tear the card up.

But I didn't.

Each person had been in the tent with Pablo when he died, Lucy included. She was the last person to talk to him, as far as I knew. Not that I would ever suspect my friend of axing someone to death.

And I did think Pablo was axed to death. Just as I knew that tomorrow would be eighty-eight degrees with four percent humidity, I knew that Pablo had been murdered. The killer had taken advantage of the tent's collapse and killed Pablo at that moment.

Now, I had five suspects for a murder that everyone thought was an accident. Everyone including my Chief of Police husband.

I was determined to keep everyone in the dark about the truth until I could finger the killer. I didn't want anyone telling me that I was wrong about Pablo's death or that I shouldn't investigate it.

And by "anyone," I meant the man I slept with.

It had been three years since I had solved a murder, but I felt right at home. Kind of like putting on an old shoe.

I slapped my credit card on the counter at Tea Time. "Latte, Ruth. And make it a double."

She slid the credit card back across the wood bar to me. "We don't take that anymore."

I slid it back toward her. "Don't mess with me today, Ruth. I've got a wicked case of PMS, I found two gray hairs this morning, and we're out of coffee at the house."

She slid the card back at me. "I'm not messing with you. Haven't you heard? The town is no longer accepting cash."

"What're you talking about?"

"It's *your* fault. So, I don't know why you don't know about it." Ruth rolled her eyes. "Remember the chicken thing?"

"The opioid theft," I supplied.

She nodded. "That's how you and I see it, but Il Moron Duce over there saw it as a referendum on cash, and he outlawed it within the city limits."

She gestured at Mayor Robinson, who was sitting at a corner table eating a cranberry scone.

I slid my card back at Ruth. "It's a credit card, Ruth. Not cash. I *need* the coffee, Ruth. Give me the coffee."

She slid the card back toward me. "Herr Idiot Himmler said cash means all American currency, and that includes your credit card."

I leaned over the bar until my face was an inch away from hers. "No. No. No. I'm pretty sure that's not legal."

"Duh. You think? Look, thems the rules, now. If you don't like it, take it up with Pol Numbskull Pot over there."

I marched to the mayor's table. "This is America," I told him. "In America, money is everything. Everything. Maybe Football, too, but mostly America is money. You're being un-American."

The mayor beamed at me, as if I had just told him that he looked ten years younger and twenty pounds lighter. "Oh, there you are. I wanted to give you your Robinson Bucks in person, since you were the inspiration for it."

He handed me a paper card, which was the size of a credit card. There was a picture of a donkey on it with "Robinson Bucks" written underneath the picture.

"From now on, you use this to pay for everything in town," he announced with pride. He was thrilled with his innovation. I was pretty excited about it, too.

"Really? I can use it for anything I want?"

He tapped the card with his index finger. "That little card is the only way you can shop within city limits from this moment onward."

I stared at the card, thinking of all the things I wanted to buy. "Wow, thank you so much."

I took the card back to Ruth. "Extra-large latte, Ruth, and give me a big slice of your cream cheese coffee cake."

She put the card in a machine, pushed some buttons, and handed the card back to me. "Are you sticking around for the Grand Opening?"

"What Grand Opening?

She waved her hand. "The mystery store next door."

I studied my fingernails in order to avoid her gaze. "I don't think so. I sort of have things to do." Ruth smiled at me. She smiled so seldom that I took a step back. "What?"

"'Things to do'? Those things wouldn't have anything to do with a certain artist and the axe in his face?"

I put my hand down and studied my shoes. "No. Of course not."

"Okay, girl. Play it that way. I won't rat you out. Holy crap, what the hell is that?"

I turned around to see what had gotten Ruth's attention. I watched through the window as two topless women with enormous breasts walked past on the sidewalk, each holding signs with *Moo!* written on them.

"Not more naked people," Ruth moaned. "I'm sick and tired of naked people. Have you noticed that this town attracts crazies? We had a long hiatus there for a while, but axes, alligators, sex dolls, and boobs have infiltrated Cannes. We're back to crazy town, Gladie."

"You forgot about Robinson Bucks," I said.

"You're right. Here. Take a second piece of cream

cheese coffee cake. I think we're going to need more fortification these days."

I took the free cake, but I no longer craved enormous quantities of food, for some reason.

Gathering my to-go cup and cake, I left Tea Time to visit Lucy. Outside, a crowd had gathered around the topless women, who were standing in front of the mystery store. A velvet curtain hung between them, hiding the store, itself. I assumed it would be removed for the Grand Opening.

The crowd waited for the big reveal, their appetites whetted—I assumed—by the topless women reveal.

I didn't want to wait for the Grand Opening of *Moo!*, but the crowd had boxed my car in, and I was stuck. The topless women started to sing "Old Macdonald had a Farm," and when they got to the *moo-moo* part, the curtains opened.

"What is it?" I heard someone ask in the crowd.

The front of the store was all pane glass windows and a sign above it said, "Moo!" And the O's in the sign looked like boobs.

I got curious, too. Lots of shops had tried to open next to Tea Time, but never a boob shop.

If that's what it was.

The door opened, and a tiny woman in a fitted

lavender suit and gobs of makeup came out. She adjusted her hair-sprayed brown hair and cleared her throat. She reminded me of Effie Trinket in *The Hunger Games*.

"What is four-hundred-times the price of crude oil?" she called to the crowd.

"Plutonium!" someone answered.

"God!" another guessed.

"My Aunt Fanny's macaroni and cheese!" another ventured, and there was a roar of laughter from the crowd.

"Wrong!" the woman called out at the top of her voice. "Breast milk. That's right. Breast milk. Breast milk is not just for babies, anymore."

Oh, geez. If this was going where I thought it was going, Spencer was definitely going to blame me for the influx of weird into his beloved town.

The crowd's laughter had stopped suddenly after the woman's comment about breast milk.

"What did that woman say?" I heard someone in the crowd ask after a minute.

"I think my hearing aid is on the blink," someone else commented.

"These days, breast milk is fortifying the greatest athletes of our time," the woman continued.

There were a few *ew's* and *gross's* uttered in the group, but it was mostly stunned silence around me. I wondered what the mayor was going to think about this. If he was against U.S. currency because it led to chicken crime, I couldn't imagine what his take on breast milk for sale would be.

On second thought, the mayor was a man, so he would probably be all in, concerning women with enormous hooters.

"Breast milk has all your necessary nutrition, and it's delicious," the woman continued with her sales pitch. "And it comes in a designer package."

The big-boobed women posed, jutting their jugs out for everyone to see. Not that anyone could miss them.

"I don't know how to feel about this," I heard a familiar voice say. I turned to find Bridget standing behind me. She pushed her glasses up on the bridge of her nose. "I feel like supporting women in however they want to use their bodies."

Bridget was the sweetest person I had ever known. She had a huge heart, and when she wasn't bookkeeping or taking care of her son, she was trying to get justice for one cause or another.

I gave her a hug. "It's a quandary," I agreed.

"Please come in for our Grand Opening," the little *Hunger Games* woman called out. "We're offering *free* samples for our first-time customers."

There was a long, awkward silence from the

crowd. All heads turned from the left to the right, like they were watching a tennis match, but I assumed they were all watching to see who among them would dare get a free sample.

Then, as if an alarm went off, the crowd surged forward toward the break milk store.

Bridget rocked from side to side, but stayed next to me. "On one hand, I should support a woman-run business," she told me. "On the other hand…"

"On the other hand, ew gross?" I finished for her. "I'm on my way to see Lucy. Do you want to go with me?"

"I'm going to stay here for a little while and determine if I need to get my sandwich board out of the trunk of my car and protest."

With the crowd now in *Moo!*, I could finally reach my car. Taking a deep breath, I opened the car door and reminded myself what I intended to do.

As far as I was concerned, Pablo Cohn had been murdered. And I was bound and determined to find out who did it.

Finally after three years, I was back on the case.

CHAPTER 8

Just like the miners that settled this town, dig deep,
dolly. Sometimes answers aren't on the surface, and you need
to dig to find out the whys and hows. In other words, the
answers are not skin deep. They want a big wedding, but
why? If you dig a little, you might find out that they only
want a big wedding because their Auntie Ida wants a big
wedding. But maybe they actually want a small wedding on
a beach in Timbuktu. If Timbuktu has a beach. What do I
know? I'm an old lady on a mountain. What do I know from
beaches? Anyway, dig a little for the answers. Dig a little for
their happiness. Dig a little so you don't have tsuris later.
— Lesson 8, Wedding Business Advice From
Your Grandma Zelda

I turned the air conditioning on in the car, as I

drove to Lucy's house. It wasn't terribly hot, but it was unbearably dry, and I hoped the air conditioning would provide some much-needed humidity.

I passed through the gate to the McMansion development and then through Uncle Harry's personal, second gate with an armed guard, who looked under my car with a mirror. Uncle Harry was in a business that he didn't talk about, but it required armed guards and a whole bunch of cigars.

I rang the doorbell and stepped back. Uncle Harry had two Rottweilers. I was terrified of them, and for good reason. Every time Uncle Harry hosted a poker game, he needed an ambulance waiting nearby.

The housekeeper opened the door, and the two Rottweilers were next to her, barking and snarling at me.

"Hi, Gladie," she greeted me. "Lucy's around back, gardening."

I blinked. "Lucy is what?"

She slapped her forehead. "Did I say gardening? I meant she's with the gardener."

There were three gardeners. One for the grass. One for the plants and flowers. And one who only blew leaves, as far as I could tell.

I found Lucy on the large deck in the back, yelling in her genteel way, at the gardener who stood under the deck, desperately holding onto the side of the hill so he wouldn't fall the long way down into the canyon.

I had fallen there once, and it wasn't pretty.

"Darlin', you clean up all that scratchy stuff," Lucy was telling the gardener. "What if one of my children fell down there and scratched themselves?"

"You mean the scrub?" the gardener called back, sounding annoyed and panicked. His foot slipped, and he scrambled to grab onto the side of the hill, again. "The whole hillside is scrub. That's part of the canyon. You don't want me to clean the *entire* hillside, right? It's acres."

Lucy adjusted her hair. "That better not be complaining I hear, darlin', or I will not stop killing you. We're talking about the safety of my children."

He grumbled something that I couldn't hear because it was drowned out when he reluctantly turned on his Weed Wacker and began to go to town, destroying the natural vegetation while trying not to fall.

Lucy was wearing a flowy peach dress with peach-colored, strappy high-heeled sandals. She was craning her head over the side of the deck, watching the gardener obey her every command.

"Hello there, Legs," I heard behind me. I turned to see Uncle Harry. He was lighting up a huge cigar and was wearing dress slacks, shiny black shoes, and a dark blue button-down shirt.

Uncle Harry had no neck, so it was always a little disarming when he turned his head. "This is a nice surprise," he told me.

"I came to see if Lucy wanted to putter around town."

It wasn't a total lie. Investigating a murder around town could have been described as "puttering." Also, I wanted to grill her about what happened in the tent, but I decided to keep that to myself.

Uncle Harry puffed on his cigar and blew out a thin tube of smoke. "She's been expecting you, or actually, she's been hoping you'd come."

"Really?"

"I'm happy you're here. Please take my wife away and distract her with murder."

"Murder?" I asked, innocently, pretending that I didn't know what he was talking about."

"C'mon, Legs. A wall of axes just happens to fall on a guy, and he gets one right in the kisser? Maybe we would have believed that if you hadn't been close by. But murder seems to bounce off you, and Lucy is all set to be your Dr. Watson."

I didn't point out that Lucy was a suspect. She had been standing next to Pablo at the time, and she had just threatened him in her sweet Southern way.

Lucy turned around and noticed me for the first time. "I'll get my handbag," she said, breathless. "And I'm driving," she added and skipped into the house.

A minute later, she came out wearing a peach silk scarf over her head and holding a designer bag. She artfully smeared a thick layer of lipstick on her lips.

"This dry weather is doing a number on my lips," she explained. "Let's go. The Mercedes is ready and waiting in the driveway.

Lucy marched around the outside of the house to the front with me following, like she was Patton.

Once we were inside her car, she revved it up, checked herself in the rearview mirror, and clutched onto the steering wheel with both hands.

"Well? Where are we going? Do you already know who killed that no-good, lecherous artist?"

"I don't have a clue who killed him," I confessed. "Maybe it was an accident, but I think we should start with Susan Chu."

Lucy gasped, like she was sucking in enough air to last her during a deep dive. "Genius, Gladie. You're a bona fide genius. Of course. Why didn't I think of that before? The bride did it."

"There's a good chance."

I needed to ask Lucy more questions about Pablo and what exactly happened in the tent, but I didn't know how to do it without accusing her of murder. Since I didn't want to offend one of my best friends, I decided to let it drop.

For now.

During our drive, after I told Lucy about the *Moo!* Grand Opening, she insisted on going through the Historic District on our way to Susan's mother's place, in order to spy on the store. As we got near, we saw steady foot traffic in and out of the new shop.

"Sweet baby Dolly Parton, that's the middle school principal walking in," Lucy cried and almost drove onto the sidewalk.

She parked on the street while she caught her breath, so she wouldn't crash the car. *Moo!* was doing bang-up business. Either that, or a breast milk shop was attracting record-numbers of lookie-loos.

Lucy clutched her steering wheel and took a deep breath, exhaling slowly. "Gladie, do you know how much I want to go in there and see what on earth they're up to?"

"A breast milk store is a curiosity," I allowed.

"But I also want to find out who killed Pablo."

It was the perfect moment to ask her for more details about what had happened in the tent, but I didn't want her to think that she was a suspect. Even though, technically she was.

"I'm sure the store will still be there tomorrow," Lucy said, like she was thinking out loud. "But the dirty dog killer could be in Boise, if we wait any longer."

Deciding on the murder instead of breast milk, she put the car into drive, just as a man ran down the center of the street. He was wild-eyed and running like an Olympic sprinter along the street's yellow, dotted lines. Lucy slammed on her brakes, as we watched him run by.

The detective Margie was running after him. "Stop! Thief! Stop in the name of the law!" she shouted, even though she was clearly out of breath.

Remington came barreling around a corner and ran down the street, too. He paused for a second when he saw me in the car and winked at me before he continued running.

"Oh, that man can uncurdle cottage cheese and turn it into Grade A cream," Lucy breathed with admiration and more than a touch of arousal.

"He has good muscle-tone," I agreed. Actually, Remington had a lot of good stuff. I had seen it all, up close and naked.

But Spencer also had a lot of good stuff, and after three years of his good stuff on a nightly basis, I was no less delighted by it.

"Remington has seven tattoos. Or was it nine?" I

said.

"Darlin', if I had ever had the pleasure of seeing his tattoos, I would never forget the count. What was that other man clutching to his chest?"

"You mean the thief they were chasing down the street? I think they were avocados."

Lucy pulled the car away from the curb. "He must have had at least a half-dozen avocados. I wish I knew where he stole them from. Harry wanted guacamole for his poker night, but the housekeeper couldn't find an avocado anywhere."

We drove to Susan's mother's place. Her mother answered the door as soon as we rang the bell, and I wondered if she was waiting for us.

"Good. There you are," she told me. I heard a familiar scream coming from upstairs. "Is that Susan?" Susan and Neil were supposed to be in their new home in San Diego. She had shown me a photo of the kitchen organizational system they had installed. It had circular drawers for utensils.

"Yes. And Neil's here, too. It's been bedlam. We're not happy with your wedding planning skills."

Lucy pushed me out of the way and got in Susan's mother's face, wagging her perfectly manicured finger with a vengeance.

"Gladie put on a gorgeous wedding for you no-account, ungrateful, lower than a snake's belly people. So, you take that back. Hurry, before I get angry."

It was nice having an attack-friend. She was just like a Pit Bull, but she didn't shed, and I never had to buy her food.

"What happened? Why is Susan here?" I asked from behind Lucy.

Susan marched down the stairs and pushed her mother and Lucy out of her way so she could stare me down with her red, swollen eyes. Her nose was running, and she wiped it with her sleeve. What was left of her mascara and eyeliner was streaked down her cheeks, and the full consequences of her home permanent were clear, now that Bird's ministrations had worn off. She was wearing a white suit, which I had assumed she had put on the day before to drive to her new home after getting married. The lapels of her blazer were stained with red Cheetos dust.

I would have recognized that stain anywhere. I had had a lot of experience with that particular kind of stain.

There was also more than a little evidence of leftover wedding cake frosting on her shirt.

"You!" she screeched at me, and a bubble of snot popped out of her left nostril. I pretended I didn't notice. "You! You! You!"

"You have to admit, she's good with pronouns," Lucy told me in an aside.

"What happened?" I asked Susan.

"You ruined my life!" she cried like a rabid bear and lunged for my throat.

Lucy slapped her hand away. "Snap out of it, missy," she ordered in her best mother-of-triplets voice.

Susan stumbled backward and clutched her slapped hand. Tears started to stream down her face. "You ruined my life," she blubbered.

"I'm sorry about the bull and the tent and the dead body," I told her honestly. I wanted to be a good wedding planner. I wanted to be part of a couple's happiest day. I was a romantic at heart, and I believed that a wedding was more than just a party.

And I wanted to make it special.

It had occurred to me more than once that it had been my fault that the bull went bonkers and that the tent fell down. But I *knew* that Pablo had been murdered, and that had nothing to do with my skills as a wedding planner.

"Not that. Here. Here! Here! Here!" Susan cried.

"That's not a pronoun," Lucy commented, tapping her chin with her index finger. "Maybe it's a preposition? I don't know. I was better in math than grammar in school."

"Your husband trapped us here," Susan yelled and burst into hysterics.

"Chief Bolton told Susan that she couldn't leave town until the investigation in that stupid artist's suspicious death was complete," Susan's mother explained.

"He what?" I asked. "He did what?"

That sneak. He had insisted that Pablo's death had been a freak accident, but he really considered it a "suspicious death." That sneak! How dare he hide the truth from me. Of course, I knew why he was hiding it from me. He didn't want his wife to get the murder bug again and tear through the town hunting down killers and getting into trouble.

But how dare he! I was a modern woman. I had kept my own name, for goodness sake. If I wanted to hunt killers and get into trouble, that was my business. How dare he!

Sure, I was hiding my investigation from him, but I *always* hid my investigations from him. That was expected behavior. Totally normal for me. If I didn't, that would be abnormal, like drinking milk upside down or wearing Spanx to an all-you-can-eat buffet.

He, on the other hand, was just a big, fat liar, and I was going to get back at him, no matter what.

"Trapped! Here! Here! Here!" Susan cried.

Neil peeked his head downstairs. He was holding a chicken leg and took a big bite out of it. He smiled at me. Friendly. "Hey there, Gladie. How's it going?"

Susan burst into more tears.

Boy, men sure are dense.

"Darlin', you need to learn how to read a room," Lucy told him.

"I didn't know that you were trapped here," I told Susan in my sweet, wedding planner voice. "Believe me, I didn't. I just came to…"

My voice faded away. I had come to find out where Susan lived so I could grill her about Pablo's murder. Actually, I was planning on pointing the finger right at her. As far as I was concerned, she was totally capable of axing a man through the face. If she was holding an axe right this second, she would have axed us all.

Susan Chu had anger issues.

Lucy clapped her hands together like a schoolmarm. "Focus. Gladie needs the rundown of what happened in the tent before Pablo was felled like a beetle-worn oak tree. Don't you know who she is? She's the Miss Marple of Cannes, California. She's the reincarnation of Sherlock Holmes, but with better style and longer hair. You need to give her the rundown. She's the town's detective."

"You were there, too. Why don't *you* tell her?" Susan demanded.

"Me?" Lucy sputtered and stammered. "I...I...I didn't see a thing. Pablo was there. Then, I turned around, and when I looked back he was going toward *you*."

She pointed her finger with a peach-painted fingernail at Susan. This was new information for me. The last I knew, Pablo had been with Lucy, she threatened him, and then the tent collapsed.

Susan's mouth dropped open, and her expression turned from sadness to anger. "That's a lie," she spat.

"Are you calling me a liar?" Lucy asked, even though it was obvious that Susan was calling her a liar.

"I didn't even talk to that artist guy, let alone put an axe through him," Susan said.

"That's true," Neil chimed in. "Susan had decided to cancel him, like she did with the check she had sent him for the painting. She turned him invisible."

"What does that mean?" I asked.

"It means he was invisible to me," Susan explained. "I couldn't see him. So, if he had gone up to me, I wouldn't have even known it."

"That's...well, I don't know what that is," Lucy said.

"It's a thing," Susan's mother explained to me.

"She makes people she doesn't like, invisible."

To illustrate, Susan snapped her fingers and pointed at me.

"Poof. You're invisible," she informed me. "And I wouldn't try to cash our check. I canceled it right after your husband told me I couldn't leave town."

Lucy started her car and poked my cheek. "Nope. You're still there. I was worried for a moment, but you're not invisible at all."

A minute after I was made invisible by my first wedding client, they closed the door on our faces, and we went back to Lucy's Mercedes.

"I thought Susan had issues because of the stress of the wedding, but the wedding's over, and she's just as batshit crazy as ever," I noted.

Lucy pulled away from the curb and drove toward the Historic District.

"I'm sorry about the check," she said. "It's not fair after all the work you did."

"Don't worry. I deposited the check the second I got it. I've already spent most of it. Don't tell Spencer."

Lucy nodded. "Girl's code, darlin'. I would never betray you."

I slapped my forehead. "Damn. I forgot I had a hair appointment with Bird."

"But it's Sunday."

"She's open today because everyone's getting dolled up for Starfest. It starts tonight."

"Oh, that's right. I bought a crystal-encrusted pair of binoculars from Tiffany's for it. I'll drop you at the salon and have one of Harry's men take your car over there, so you'll have it after your appointment. This was fun. I'm going to invest in some equipment for our investigation. I think Susan did it. Invisible, my ass."

The salon was packed. Normally, Bird worked on two or three customers at once. She would stagger them so she would have one getting shampooed while she put another's color on and yet another would be under the blow dryer.

But today, Bird was already working on five customers at a time when I walked in. The other hairdressers were struggling to keep up, and the manicurists and pedicurists were going at cuticles like General Beauregard at the Battle of Bull Run.

There had been a sad lack of community events over the summer because of budget cuts, due to problems with the sewage system. Now, Cannes residents were going over the top to celebrate Starfest before the summer ended.

Even though it was going to be held at night up

in the mountains, women still wanted smooth heels and no gray roots.

"Take a seat, Gladie," Bird called and waved a dye brush at a chair where an elderly lady was sitting. "Move it, Courtney. Grab a coffee in back. You've got another fifteen minutes before I pull your color through."

"Coffee gives me the runs," Courtney complained.

"All the better," Bird said. "It'll help you get back into the dress you want to wear tonight."

Courtney smiled at the idea of wearing her dress, and vacated the chair. I took a seat and caught my reflection in the mirror. I had looked better, but I had also looked worse. My frizzy hair was all over the place, but I had done a good job with my mascara and eye shadow.

Bird slapped a smock around me. "What're we doing today?"

"I don't' know. You told me I had to come in."

"Oh, that's right. You need highlights. Your new job has got you looking haggard."

"It has?" I asked, alarmed.

Bird studied me a second. "But you don't look haggard today. You have a glow about you. Are you pregnant?"

"No. Why does everyone keep asking me that?"

Bird ignored my question. "And I'm not letting you leave here without getting your mustache waxed."

My hand flew to my upper lip. "My mustache?"

"Not really a mustache. Just some dark hairs there. A lot of them. Like a seventies porn star."

I leaned forward to better look at my mustache in the mirror. "You're brutally honest, Bird."

"Honey, in my business, I have to be. I could get sued if I let a woman leave here with a mustache or scraggy heels." She began to apply the color with tin foil packets wrapped around strands of my hair. "I'm so glad I have a normal person to work on. There's been a real influx of crazy around here."

"What kind of crazy?"

Bird was the ears of the town. It was conceivable that she had heard something important about the murder.

She pulled her gloves off. "That *Moo!* store. I've seen things today that I never thought I'd see. Breasts are everywhere. Big honkers. Leaking ones."

"Ouch!" a woman shouted in a chair behind me. She jumped up, scaring her hairdresser. She was wearing a tight t-shirt and no bra. Her large, pendulous breasts had leaked through her shirt, just like Bird had described a second before.

"See? See?" Bird whispered to me. "It's been like

that. *Moo!* is the right name. We could make yogurt for days with what's going on."

The leaking woman screamed at the hairdresser, and the hairdresser screamed back at her. The rest of the salon had stopped what they were doing and had turned to witness the action.

It was getting heated. Bird issued a stern warning to the woman, but she didn't seem to hear. Or she didn't want to hear.

That's when the hair-pulling started, and for some crazy reason that I'll never understand, I stood and walked over to them.

"Can't we all just be friends?" I asked.

And that's when it happened.

CHAPTER 9

Love is like a kick in the head. It leaves a mark. You know what I mean, bubbeleh? Any shayna punim can turn a sane man crazy. Crazy in love. The best kind of meshugana. Use that crazy. Use that kick in the head. Use it as a reminder when the meshugana gets cold feet. Remind him about his mark. Remind him about what he wants.

— Lesson 9, Wedding Business Advice From Your Grandma Zelda

I don't know why I said that. I don't know why I wanted everyone to be friends. I mean, not everyone is friends with everyone. That would be too many friends. It would be chaos with the Christmas presents, alone.

Total bedlam.

But despite my obsessive interest in murdered

people, I didn't like to see violence or conflict.

Now the leaking woman was pulling her hairdresser's hair, and Bird had gotten involved because hair-pulling—especially in a salon—was sacrilegious for a hairdresser.

Bird had strong, toned arms from decades of working on hair, but she was no match for the woman with the milk-stained shirt. That woman was a banshee. A wild tiger bent on revenge. It wasn't clear what had set her off. I thought it had something to do with the hair extensions she was getting.

But maybe it was just hormones from the breastfeeding.

"Can't we all just be friends?" I asked again.

The woman kneed the hairdresser in her privates, and she flew backward.

"Hey!" Bird yelled. "That's my best hair and eyelash extension technician. You better not have injured her."

In reply, the woman went for Bird, but Bird was quick. She retaliated hard.

Wow, there sure was a lot of anger going around. Susan was a ball of anger and now even the salon, which had always been the center of the sisterhood community based on harmless vanity, had been infected with it.

Where was my peace? Where was my serenity?

This was a salon. There wasn't supposed to be fighting in hair care.

"Can't we all just be friends?" I repeated.

"She's got my hair!" Bird screeched. "She's got my hair! I can't believe you're going for *my* hair in *my* salon!"

I got nearer to the fray. "Can't we all just be friends?" I asked, again, even though I was pretty sure of the answer.

"Shut up!" The woman and Bird yelled in unison.

The woman let go of Bird for a second, lifted her shirt, and squeezed one of her breasts. I couldn't believe what I was seeing, even though my eyes had widened to twice their normal size.

The woman squeezed, and in an instant, milk squirted out. Bird dodged the stream, but I was right in its path. With amazing speed and shocking force, the milk hit me in one eye, and when I flinched from the impact, it hit my other eye.

"Hey, that's one of my regular customers!" I heard Bird yell, coming to my defense. My eyes were shut tight. There was the sound of a loud grunt, then running, and then cheers from the salon.

"Yay, Bird!" I heard.

"I'm blind," I cried.

"That was amazing, Bird. You really let her have

it," I heard someone else say.

"I can't see," I cried. "I'm blind."

"You saved the day. Did you see how that lunatic ran out of here when you shoved her?" I heard another customer say.

There was another round of applause to cheer on Bird's shoving ability.

"I've been milked," I cried, getting desperate. I felt a major panic attack coming on. "The breast milk is burning my eyes. Burning. Blind. Boobs. Help."

In a salon filled with women, there was a lot of institutional knowledge about breast milk, and every single one of them was sure that breast milk couldn't blind me or even sting my eyes. At least that's what they told me when they finally noticed me standing in the center of the salon, my eyes stinging and swollen shut.

"Help. Milk. Burning," I said.

Someone took me by the elbow to the bathroom. I felt around for the sink, and I flushed my eyes with cold water. There was a noise in the salon, and the person who was with me left the bathroom to see what was happening.

The water didn't do any good. I could crack my eyes open a tiny bit, but I was still in pain, and I could only see light with no form. I felt around for the door and walked out.

"I'm still blind," I announced.

"Ma'am, this woman claims that you physically assaulted her," I heard. I recognized Remington's voice, and for a moment, I thought he was talking to me, but he sounded like he was on the other side of the salon, and Bird responded to him, so I assumed he was talking to her.

"I did not. The woman's crazy. She milked Gladie," Bird told Remington.

"She…what did you say?" Remington asked.

"Help. Blind. Eyes. Milk," I said.

Despite a salon full of women on Bird's side, the milk-woman had a large bruise, and the *Hunger Games* woman from *Moo!* on *her* side. Remington took Bird to the police station to question her, and someone sat me in a chair and gave me a cold compress to put on my eyes while I listened to the gossip.

Most of it centered around *Moo!* and its army of breastfeeding women who were making a fortune in the breast milk pyramid scheme, which allowed them to afford liposuction and salon treatments.

"It's not normal, a whole army of women with a thigh gap," a customer commented about the liposuctioned breast milkers.

"Communists," another customer said, like she had inside information on Communist pyramid schemes.

But some of the gossip had to do with Pablo and his house, and my ears perked up when I heard it.

"Cursed house. He should never have moved in," I heard.

"I heard the bride killed him," someone else commented.

"I heard it was the best man with the muscles who did it. The guy drinks too much and gets into fistfights," someone else said.

She was talking about Brian Bishop. He was on my suspect list. He had been drinking, and he had seemed capable of violence, but not as violent as a communist breast milk provider getting rich from a pyramid scheme.

The problem with Brian Bishop was that he lived in San Diego, and I didn't know how to find him. Since I was invisible, I didn't think Susan would help me.

After fifteen minutes with the cold compress on my eyes, the talk changed when the door opened and someone walked in.

"It's the cop. The one with the body," I heard.

"Nobody fills out a suit like him. He's like James Bond but with better hair," someone else said.

It was Spencer, of course. He had come to save me. The good news was now I could get home safely. The bad news was that Spencer would never let me live this down. And how could he? Getting blinded by breast milk was one of those never-live-down kind of events.

I heard his designer shoes approach, and then I could feel his warmth in front of me and smell his delicious cologne.

"Remington told me to pick you up, but he didn't tell me why," he said.

"I was milked," I said.

"You were milked," he said, like he was reciting the weather.

"Squirted."

"Squirted."

"She squeezed a boob, and *pow!* she got me in both eyes."

"She squeezed a boob, and *pow!* she got you in both eyes."

"Would you please stop repeating everything I say?" I asked, annoyed. I pressed the compress harder over my eyes.

"I'm sorry," Spencer said. "I understand the words coming out of your mouth, but I wasn't sure about the order."

"Breast milk is burning holes in my eyes," I said, enunciating every word.

"Breast milk is burning holes in your eyes," Spencer repeated.

"You're doing it, again."

"Sorry."

"Breast milk isn't acidic," a woman in curlers interrupted. "It wouldn't hurt your eyes, especially after rinsing them out. I think your wife just got scared. The boobie woman was scary."

"Hear that, Pinky?" Spencer asked. "You were just scared of the boobie woman."

Maybe they were right. Breast milk couldn't do damage to my eyes. It was probably psychosomatic. Totally in my mind. I took the compress off and tried to crack my eyes open.

"You're right," I said. "I can almost open them all the way."

The woman in curlers screamed, and Spencer stepped backward, his hand over his open mouth.

"What? What is it?" I asked.

Turning the chair around, I looked at myself in the mirror. My eyes were rimmed with red, swollen circles, and the whites of my eyes had disappeared. There was only red.

I had no more whites.

"I have no more whites," I breathed.

Spencer drove us home from the local clinic. They had flushed my eyes and given me a shot of

Benadryl, which had made me slightly loopy.

None of it worked.

"I can't believe you're allergic to breast milk," Spencer said, laughing.

"It's not funny. I should have been warned that breast milk is dangerous. There should be a warning on those women's breasts, like the warning on a pack of cigarettes."

"What I don't get is the tin foil. Is that a new style? Or are you trying to contact Mars?"

My hands flew to my head. Bird had never taken out the foil packets after she did the highlights. I had forgotten all about them.

"Oh my God. It's been hours," I moaned. "My hair is going to be fried."

"I'm pretending that this isn't happening," Spencer told me as he drove. "See my smiling face? This is the smiling face of a contented man, a man who's not living in a tornado of weird."

"I'm not sure you're insulting me, but I have a feeling."

"No, it's not you. You're in the tornado, too. You've been swept up in it with me."

"That's true. It's not my fault," I said and didn't tell him that I was actively investigating Pablo's murder.

Spencer dropped me at home. Grandma was

waiting for me in the open doorway.

"I heard," she said. "I saw a pair of breasts, but I thought my radar was wonky."

"No, your radar is on target. There were breasts. Evil, evil breasts."

I went upstairs and washed what was left of my hair. Then, I pulled it back in a ponytail and slipped a pair of sunglasses on, even though it was almost dark out.

Downstairs, Ruth and my grandmother were waiting for me. Grandma was wearing a knockoff Diane von Furstenberg jumpsuit, which was two sizes too small, and Ruth was wearing a long, red velvet dress with work boots.

"Damn. You covered the damage. I heard it was bad," Ruth said.

I took my sunglasses off to show her the damage. She gasped, sucking air through her teeth. "That's from breast milk? Those breasts should come with a warning label, like on a pack of cigarettes."

Whoa. It was the same thing that I had said a few minutes before. Any similarities between Ruth and me scared me.

"Don't be ridiculous," I said. "That's a crazy thing to say."

Since Spencer was on duty, I accompanied Ruth and Grandma to Starfest. Grandma was on the committee and needed to be there early. Ruth was just a fan of stars. She said she liked the idea of being in space where no one could bother her.

Ruth drove and parked her car in a makeshift parking lot by a large meadow, high in the mountains. Long folding tables had already been set up, and local merchants were putting out food, drinks, and blankets to sell.

"My eyes better be tricking me," Ruth grumbled. "Because if that's Debra Stone putting out a teapot, I will flail her alive."

"You don't have a monopoly on tea, Ruth," Grandma pointed out.

"Big talk, Zelda. I remember you weren't so pleased when a rival matchmaker came to town."

"I welcomed the help to spread love to the masses," Grandma said, looking at her hands. "I want brownies. I hope Debra's selling brownies to go with that tea."

We got out of the car and walked over to the table. It was already dark out, and they had put out downward-facing lights to illuminate the tables and footpaths without obstructing the view of the stars. Later on, when everyone was in place in the meadow, even those lights would be turned off, so we could get the full effect.

Wearing my sunglasses, I couldn't see much, and I kept tripping over rocks.

"Debra, put away that teapot," Ruth growled.

"You can't bully me, Ruth Fletcher," Debra said, sounding like she was being bullied.

I didn't want to witness another argument, so I moved on to the other tables. There were mostly desserts and hot apple cider for sale, but Bernie's Rib Shack had set up two tables with its full dinner menu. At the end of the line of tables, there were three side to side, piled high with apple pies.

Staring at those tables, a feeling of dread hit me, but I couldn't figure out why. My radar had been wonky lately. It hadn't warned me about the chicken, the Crisco, or the breast milk, for example. Let alone Pablo's murder.

But my third eye was like that. It liked to focus on other people's lives. Not mine. Still, the icy dread crept up my spine, and I didn't know why.

While I tried to figure it out, Brian Bishop walked by. He was heading for the barbecue tables. He looked pleased as punch. The last time I had seen him, he was spitting mad at Pablo.

Jackpot!

I never thought I could find him, but here he was, practically dropped in my lap. Walking casually, I sidled up next to Brian.

"This looks good," I said, nonchalantly.

He turned toward me in surprise, and then he smiled at me like Wile E. Coyote finally catching the roadrunner.

"Hello." He dragged out the word, turning it into four syllables.

Yuck. He was a frat boy who played with tractors and couldn't hold his liquor. But he was also one of my suspects, so I smiled back at him.

"Hello. I thought you'd be back in San Diego by now."

He leaned his hand on the table and stared at my chest. "Maybe I wanted to be closer to you."

Blech. He was gross. It wasn't that he was unattractive because he was very nice looking, but he made my skin crawl.

"That's sweet of you," I said.

"Hey, do you have one of those Robinson Bucks cards? They won't take anything else, and I'm starved."

"Uh…Sure." I handed him my card.

He ordered himself a rack of ribs, potato salad, and a beer. Then, he handed me back the card.

"So, Pablo," I started.

"What a pig. He was lucky he got axed in the face because I would have really let him have it."

I didn't know what to say to that. What was

worse than getting axed in the face?

"Weird about the axe," I noted. "Did you see it happen?"

"Nah. I was talking to the catering chick."

"Debbie?"

"Is that her name? Do you have her number? I mean, if you and I aren't going to happen."

We weren't going to happen. We were so not going to happen. Aliens invading would happen sooner. A ninety-percent off sale at Saks Fifth Avenue would happen sooner.

"So, you were with Debbie? Was that far away from Pablo?"

He shrugged and took a bite of his ribs. "Actually, she walked away just before the tent came down. You know what? I saw her talking to Pablo right before that happened."

"Debbie was next to Pablo?"

"Yep. So, how about you and me?"

I was about to ask him another question when I realized why the tables of apple pies had provoked a feeling of dread.

I turned around to look at them, again. The apple pies were a huge draw. They were surrounded by townspeople, handing over their Robinson Bucks cards for a slice of apple pie.

I waved my hands at them. "Get back! Get away! Save yourself!" I yelled.

They looked at me like I was crazy, and why wouldn't they? I was warning them away from delicious apple pie.

"Those pies are dangerous!" I continued. "Hurry! Run for your lives!"

They ignored me, but they noticed when the trees shook nearby.

"Hurry!" I urged. "Save yourselves!"

I launched myself forward and started to throw the apple pies away from the tables toward the trees. But it was no use.

The giant, stolen, San Diego Zoo alligator burst from the trees in a gallop.

And he looked like he had a hankering for apple pie.

CHAPTER 10

Step by step. That's how things get done, bubbeleh. That's why walking down the aisle is so important in a wedding. It's taking those last little steps to commitment. So, make the aisle pretty. Make it wide so it can fit the bride's parents. There's nothing worse than a narrow aisle. It's like bad sex. Not that I know anything about bad sex. Anyway, remember the steps. They lead to resolution.

— Lesson 10, Wedding Business Advice From
Your Grandma Zelda

A wave of retirees jumped away from the apple pie tables, just in time. Amazingly, the alligator looked even bigger than before, but with my injured eyes and dark sunglasses, I couldn't be sure.

All I was sure about was that the alligator was big,

that it could run surprisingly fast on its short, stubby legs, and that it was about to eat a bunch of Starfest attendees along with some apple pies.

"Alligator! Out of the way!"

I grabbed several pies and threw them at the alligator in hopes that he would pause in order to eat them and give the stunned people a chance to escape. But the alligator wasn't a pie-in-the-hand-is-worth-two-in-the-bush kind of alligator. He was an all-or-nothing kind of alligator, and he was going for all.

Only a couple seconds had passed, and I realized that not only had I failed in stopping the alligator's trajectory, but that I was right in his trajectory. I was standing between the alligator and its sweet tooth's desire.

Somebody screamed.

I think it was me.

My life passed before my eyes like a movie. A very short movie. More like the five-minute cartoon before a movie.

Damn it. I didn't want to be a five-minute cartoon. I wanted to be a movie. A long one with an intermission so I could pee.

I shut my injured eyes and waited for the imminent attack because I didn't want to see it coming, and I didn't have enough time to jump out of the way.

Suddenly, there was an unearthly scream.

Like Tarzan.

I opened my eyes to see an Armani suit burst through the trees and practically fly through the air in my direction.

No, not my direction.

The alligator's direction.

It was Spencer. My Spencer. He had come to save me.

He yelled one more time, and then he was on top of the alligator with his arms around its throat.

"I've got it!" Spencer called.

The alligator stopped running and thrashed against its captor, but Spencer managed to hold on, as if he was a champion rodeo rider.

"I've got it!" he called again, but this time he didn't sound as sure of himself. "Holy crap, I'm wrestling an alligator!" he yelled, like he had just figured out that fact.

"Somebody shoot it!" somebody screamed.

I think it was me.

"No! It's endangered!" Spencer yelled.

The alligator whipped its body so hard that Spencer was flung into the air and landed on one of the apple pie tables. Defeated, or rather frustrated, the alligator slinked back into the forest without eating one slice of the apple pies.

I knew how it felt. Diets are a bitch.

Checking on Spencer, I took off my sunglasses and leaned over his body on the table, looking for signs of life.

"I wrestled an alligator," he said.

"You saved me."

"I did? Boy, I'm a hero. Maybe now you'll do that thing I want."

"You're four years old."

Starfest continued without apple pies or an alligator. Spencer seemed unharmed, but the paramedics checked him out, anyway. While they were doing that, I looked around for Brian, but by that time, the lights were out, and it was hard to make out anybody in the group of stargazers.

That's how come I didn't see the skateboarders until I ran into them.

"Hey, it's the babe," the leader said.

"Yeah, the babe."

"The babe. Yeah."

"Bitchin'. The babe."

They had their delivery bags with them, and they were eating out of them. I asked if they had seen Brian, but they didn't know him, and when I explained that he had been at the wedding and I wanted to talk to him about Pablo's death, the lead skateboarder dropped his handful of ill-gotten fries and perked up.

"Dude, I saw that guy," he said.

"That's right. Like, we did," another of them said.

"You saw Brian?" I asked. "Where?"

"No, not *your* dude. The other dude. The one with the axe in his head."

They proceeded to alternately mime getting axed and axing someone.

"Where?" I asked, interrupting their show. "At the wedding? Did you see him die?" It was too much to ask for, but stranger things were known to happen.

"No, dude. Like, before."

"The day before."

"Yeah, dudette. We saw him the day before."

"Where?" I asked. "What was he doing?"

The head skateboarder stepped closer to me and lowered his voice. "That's the thing. He was acting real shady. Skulking around. You know?"

"He was skulking?"

"Yeah. Skulking."

"Where?" I asked, again.

And that's when their drug-addled brain cells stopped working. Like a case of communal amnesia, they couldn't remember where they had seen Pablo "skulk."

That word made me very suspicious. Pablo hadn't been a skulker. He had always wanted to be the center of attention. So, why was he skulking the day before he was murdered?

The next morning, Spencer and I slept in. Spencer was sore from wrestling an alligator, and my eyes were no longer painful, but they were still red and swollen.

At eight o'clock, we were still spooning in bed, and Spencer's lips were against the crook of my shoulders, kissing me lightly.

"We should go downstairs and toast a bagel for Zelda," he said like a good grandson-in-law. But I noticed he didn't move a muscle.

"She wasn't in the mood for bagels, so she ate leftover fried chicken an hour ago and washed it down with a cup of coffee and a Bloody Mary chaser."

"How do you know that? Never mind. I don't know why I still ask you."

Spencer's phone rang, and he stretched his arm backward to retrieve it off his nightstand.

"Bolton," he answered. "Are you kidding me? Can't you handle that on your own? What? Are you kidding me?"

Spencer hung up and rolled out of bed.

"What's happening?" I asked.

He slipped on a pair of pants. "I have to go into work right now."

"Alligator?"

"No."

"Aggressive lactation experts?"

"No."

"More sex dolls?"

"No."

I tapped my chin with a finger. "I think that's the whole list of weird going on. Oh, wait a minute. Could it be avocados?"

Spencer was halfway dressed and stopped what he was doing to look at me. "How'd you know?"

I shrugged. "Lucky guess."

He kissed me and walked to the door. "Don't get into trouble today."

"Hey, right back at you, alligator wrestler."

As soon as he left, I took a two-minute shower and ran downstairs, taking them two steps at a time. Grandma was waiting at the bottom for me with a sack breakfast and a cup of coffee.

"Here you go, dolly. Sustenance for your investigation. Where are you going first?"

I took the food and coffee from her and gave her a kiss on the cheek. "I'm going to see Debbie Porter before she leaves for work. She had a flat tire, but it's getting fixed right now."

"Yes, that's what I saw, too. You have twelve minutes to get there."

I got there in nine minutes. AAA was just finishing with her tire. Debbie seemed honestly happy to see me. She waved at me to come into the garage with her. Clear plastic bins lined two walls, each neatly tagged. The rest of the garage was neat and organized, too, and she had two washing machines and two dryers going, filled with table linens.

"Are you here to talk about the next job?" she asked.

I wanted to say, yes. She was such a nice and competent woman, and I needed to work with her to have a successful business. I gnawed on the inside of my cheek and studied a spot on a wall.

"Oh, I get it," she said. "You want to talk about our *last* job. I sort of expected that you'd be coming around. I heard how you get into murders."

I perked up. "So, you think it was a murder?"

"Not at first, but after a while, the coincidence of it rubbed me wrong."

"The coincidence?"

"You know, the odds. I mean, if it was an

accident, it was a *freak* accident. And besides, if I wanted Pablo dead, I bet everyone in that tent also wanted him dead. He was such a jerk."

I could feel one of my eyebrows arch into my hairline, but I was powerless to stop it. "You wanted him dead? He mentioned you owed him money."

Debbie leaned close to me. "This is between you and me and nobody else. Okay?"

Uh-oh. I was terrible at keeping secrets. The worst. After all, my whole thing was revealing secrets. But something told me to promise her and keep my promise. I nodded.

"After my divorce, I was desperate for money," she told me in a whisper. "Pablo gave me ten thousand dollars to pose for him."

"Wow, that's a lot of money."

"Well, it wasn't for regular paintings. It was for sick, twisted paintings that my children could never know about. I took the money, but I chickened out. I never posed for him."

"Oh."

"I was going to pay the money back, Gladie. I swear it. Business has just picked up, and I was going to go to him with a payment plan proposal. But he got axed before I could."

He got axed, which left her off the hook for ten-thousand smackeroos. That was quite an incentive to axe a man. Damn. I didn't want to lose my caterer.

"What happened in the tent?" I asked. "Did you talk to Pablo before it happened?"

"Me? No, I was working. I saw him with your friend Lucy, and then I think he tried to flirt with the bride again."

"He did? He was with Susan when the tent came down?"

Debbie seemed to think about that for a moment. "There was a little dust-up with the hot groomsman, I think, but I can't remember if that was before he talked to Susan or after."

"Brian," I breathed. That was the hot groomsman she was talking about. He was the most likely of them to axe a man. Although Susan was even more of a hothead than he was. And Lucy? I hated that everyone kept mentioning her. "Is that it? Is that all you saw?"

"Yep. Colin served him a mini-crab cake, and then the tent came down."

I froze. "Colin?"

Debbie's face widened with awareness. "Yes! That's right. Colin was right there. He probably saw something."

I had already spoken to Colin, and he had said that Lucy had been with Pablo right before the tent's collapse. He hadn't said a word about crab cakes.

"Colin's going to be at my next gig, if you want to talk to him," Debbie offered. "It's a simple brunch. I was lucky to get Colin for it. He usually tastes dog food for a living. Serving is just a side gig for him."

"I'll follow you there," I said.

We walked a few steps, and Debbie stopped. "I think you've got something in your eyes."

"Breast milk," I explained.

She nodded, sadly. "Yep. That stuff's brutal."

CHAPTER 11

Eureka! I found it! Did you know that that was first said by Shlomo the Butcher in Odessa about a hundred and fifty years ago? He was a very large man, and he hadn't seen his pupik in years. Then, one day he realized that he missed it, and he went looking. It took some work, but he found it. Anyway, a person can go for a long time not seeing something and not remembering that they miss it. It's kind of like the blind spot when you're driving. You might be driving next to a Volkswagen for miles and not know it's there, but you need to know it's there because if you change lanes, you're going to have a nasty surprise. Don't get caught with nasty surprises, bubbeleh. Always look for your pupik.

— Lesson 11, Wedding Business Advice From Your Grandma Zelda

The brunch was being held in the backyard of a large house in the Historic District. I followed Debbie's van there. Once we arrived, she immediately got into her caterer mode, and I tried to be unobtrusive so I could spy.

Watching as the workers emptied the van, I saw two guys pick their noses. It wasn't very professional, but it was understandable, considering the dry weather.

"Yowza!" one of them yelled. "The damned thing shocked me, again."

That was another downside to the dry weather: Electric shocks. I couldn't touch any metal lately without getting a shock.

There were four workers, in addition to Debbie. Two men and two women. Colin was uber-competent as usual, friendly and relaxed. I watched until they had set up the tables and chairs, and then I cornered Colin by a hedge.

"Do you remember anything else about the tent?" I asked without preamble. I had decided to take the direct route because I was getting impatient. Everyone was pointing the finger at everyone else, but even that didn't reveal any fights or arguments that took place in the tent before it collapsed. I didn't have a single clue, let alone proof, and I was getting nowhere fast.

"Oh…hi. No, I don't think so."

"Debbie told me that you were serving Pablo right before the tent came down."

If I had had a bright light, I would have shined it on Colin's face. I meant business.

"I did?" he asked.

"Yes. Mini crab cakes."

"Mini crab cakes," he said, like he was trying to remember. "Maybe," he said like a question. "But I think that was before."

"Before he was talking to the bride? To the best man?"

Colin shook his head. "No, I'm pretty sure he was with the Southern woman when the tent collapsed."

My heart sank. I had thought that Lucy was in the clear, but now here she was again, front and center as a major suspect.

Not that I suspected her.

"Pablo was a jerk to you," I noted.

"I'm used to it in my job."

"But he was particularly jerky. Mean. He treated you like dirt."

"That's true. He was an asshole. But I didn't spit in his food, and I didn't kill him. Prison isn't worth it."

Colin left to return to his work, and I stood by the hedge and tried to figure out the murder. Lucy had said that Pablo had been with Susan right before the tent collapsed. Susan had said that Pablo had been with Lucy. Brian had said that Pablo had been with Debbie, and Debbie had said that Pablo had been with Colin. Now, Colin said that Pablo had been with Lucy.

That was two for Lucy and one for everyone else.

Out of the corner of my eye, I saw a movement in the hedge, and I jumped back in a blind panic. I looked around for a weapon in case the alligator was there and going to attack. But it wasn't the alligator.

Bridget and Lucy stepped out of the hedge. They were dressed entirely in black, including black ski masks.

"Shh," Bridget said. "We're undercover."

"We're stalking the caterers, darlin'. It's always the caterers."

I gave Lucy a big hug. There was no way she could have killed Pablo. Not my Lucy.

"I've never felt more alive," Bridget said, adjusting her ski mask. "Invigorated."

Lucy nodded. "I brought pepper spray. I hope I get to use it."

"We had one of those things that can listen in to conversations from a mile away, but it got lost in the bushes," Bridget said with disappointment. "We're your backup team," she explained. "We're doing reconnaissance, and then we're going to report back to you."

"I thought you were going to protest at *Moo!*."

"I couldn't decide which way to land on *Moo!* So, I decided to join Lucy in hunting the killer."

"Did you hear what happened with Susan Chu?" Lucy asked.

I stood up straighter, and a zing of excitement rushed through me. "No. What?"

"She and Neil tried to sneak out of town," Lucy recounted. "They caught them smuggling out their two-hundred gifts, half a wedding cake, and thirty mini crab cakes. Spencer arrested them this morning."

I stomped my foot on the ground. "That fink! He told me he was on an avocado case."

"There's an avocado shortage, and people are panicking," Bridget said. "That's understandable. Avocados are a healthy fat and delicious on toast and in salads. The shortage is all because of global warming. I'm going to protest the environment after we bring the killer to justice. I ordered a new sandwich board from Amazon to do it. And after I protest the environment, I'm going to protest Amazon. Someone's got to stop them."

I said goodbye to my friends and wished them good luck. I watched them disappear into the hedge. The bushes moved, as they traveled the perimeter of the backyard.

I hoped they would find out something because I

had had no luck. I was no closer to solving the mystery. *If* there was a mystery. It could have been a freak accident.

I wasn't any closer to solving it than I had been at the time of Pablo's death. All I knew was that Susan hated Pablo because of his painting, and she didn't want to pay him for it. Brian hated Pablo because he had flirted with his best friend's bride. Debbie hated Pablo because he wanted his ten-thousand dollars back and wanted her to pose naked. Colin hated Pablo because he was an asshole to him. And Lucy? She hated Pablo because he was a disgusting lech.

None of those were the greatest motives. But if it had been a murder, it wasn't the pre-meditated kind. It was the kind that took advantage of the moment. The crime of passion kind.

Ugh. I needed more coffee.

I slapped my Robinson Bucks card on the bar. "Latte, Ruth, and make it a double. Where is everybody?"

Tea Time was a tomb. I was the only customer.

Ruth pointed to her left. "They're at the milk bar next door, getting a shot of antioxidant grossness."

I threw up a little in my mouth. "No way."

"Way. This town went from zero to sixty in the weird department. I can't look at anyone in the eye anymore—nothing personal—because they're all freaks.

I've lived in this town since Hoover was in the White House. Hoover, Gladie. Hoover. But I think I need to find a saner place to live. You know, like Milwaukee or Bethesda."

She made me a latte and told me that she was closing up the shop for a few minutes so she could do some shopping. Since I was at a dead-end with my snooping and we needed Ziploc bags, AA batteries, and eggs at home, I decided to go with her.

Pete's market was located on the eastern edge of the Historic District, next to Dave's Dry Cleaning & Tackle Shop.

Ruth drove us there, and we got two carts outside and rolled them into the store. Pete was doing better than Ruth this morning. There was a good-sized crowd of customers. Every aisle had a couple shoppers in it, and when Ruth and I finished our shopping, there was quite a line in front of us at the checkout.

"Look at this craziness with the bags," Ruth said, pointing a finger at the cashier. Recently, plastic bags had started to cost ten-cents each, in order to encourage customers to bring their own, reusable non-plastic bags.

I always forgot my bags, like I did today. So did the guy at the front of the line. He declined a bag, paid for his groceries with his Robinson Bucks card, and grabbed all of his purchases in his arms. He took two steps, and a jar of pasta sauce fell out of his arms and crashed onto the floor.

"A bag is a dime, Arthur," Ruth yelled at him. "A lousy dime. Pay the dime next time. Crazy people can't pay a dime?"

"Maybe he wants to save the environment," someone in line suggested.

"Arthur Simpleton?" Ruth shot back. "He still uses coal to heat his house, and I saw him pouring kerosene into the lake."

The next customer had remembered her reusable bags. In fact, she had brought at least a dozen of them, but the cashier stuffed all of her groceries into one single bag.

"See?" Ruth said to me. She was almost frothing at the mouth with anger. "They monetized the bags, and so now they stuff everything into one bag, like they're trying to save money even though they already have the bags. Now, her bread is under the tomatoes, under the watermelon. And none of her other bags are being used. How does that make sense? How?"

A few more customers checked out, and then there was only one more before Ruth.

"I couldn't find any avocados," the woman told the checker.

"There's an avocado shortage," the customer

behind me told her. "It's like finding a single man over fifty without a mental disorder these days. No dice."

"I haven't had avocado toast in three days," the woman at the checkout complained. "I like to eat avocado toast every morning."

Ruth elbowed me in the side. "Get her with the 'avocado toast'. Listen, lady," she called. "I've lived in Southern California my entire life. And during all those years—and I'm talking about dog's years, okay?—I've eaten toast with avocado on it. The first time I heard 'avocado toast,' I thought: toast that tastes like an avocado? Why not just put avocado on regular toast? Boy, people ruin everything."

"Modern life's sure got you down, Ruth," I noted.

She nodded. "Ever since Twitter was invented, I haven't had a moment of peace."

"Maybe you should run for political office," I suggested. "You could change things."

"And *lead* these morons? No, thank you."

"We've got some avocados secured in the back room," the cashier told the woman. "Go help yourself."

The woman left with her cart and her groceries, and we moved up to the front.

"Now, listen to me," Ruth told the cashier, plopping her reusable bags on the counter. "I want you to bag my groceries the old-fashioned way. Don't shove everything into one bag. I gave you plenty of bags so that you can pack each of them nice and light. Hear that? Nice and light. I don't have any discs left between my vertebrae, so carrying two pasta jars and a carton of milk in a single bag will send me straight to the hospital. And while I'm at it, the woman behind me is paying for her bags. She can afford a few dimes, and give her paper bags instead of plastic. Save the damned whales, why don't you."

There was a loud scream. At first, I thought I was the one screaming because of frustration from shopping with Ruth, but the scream had come from the back of the store.

The back of the store where the avocados were hidden.

A man dressed in shorts, a t-shirt, and a chicken head ran to the front of the store, holding at least a dozen avocados in his arms. One of them fell to the floor and rolled under the canned goods aisle.

"He must have forgotten his reusable bags," Ruth commented.

"Stand back!" the avocado thief growled. He must have found the chicken head in the alley after the other chicken thief had taken it off to get high.

The costume wasn't as effective with only the

head.

"Will, is that you? I recognize your knees," the woman behind me asked him.

"I deserve avocado toast," the thief replied and ran out of the store. Nobody followed him. Without a licorice gun, it was sort of anti-climactic.

Ruth and I paid with our Robinson Bucks cards, and as we were leaving, Pete stopped Ruth.

"Have you gotten any actual money from this Robinson Bucks thing?" he asked her.

"No, but it's only been a couple days. Why?"

"Because it's all fishy to me. There's no actual number to call, no money transferred into my bank, and I think those Robinson Bucks machines don't communicate with a real place. And the paper cards? No magnetic strip on them."

After her conversation with Pete, Ruth grumbled under her breath all the way to her car. We packed the groceries into her trunk and got in the car.

"It's finally happened, Gladie," Ruth said, staring straight ahead. "I've become one of the morons. I can't believe I let that fool mayor trick me into using his crap cards. I should be tarred and feathered."

"Don't blame the victim, Ruth."

"Why not? Sometimes the victim deserves it."

A lightning bolt went through me, and I saw a

bright light of epiphany. It was an ah-ha moment. A why-have-I-been-so-stupid event.

I had been looking at Pablo's murder all wrong. I had been focused on the suspects and had gotten nowhere.

I should have been focused on the victim.

Grandma and I sat down for lunch after her morning "Dating Do's and Don't's" class was over. Meryl had dropped by during her lunch hour from the library, and we all enjoyed a lunch of Herbie's Hoagies and potato chips with vanilla cream soda to wash it down.

After, I cleaned the kitchen, while my grandmother and Meryl drank a cup of tea.

"I think I'll stretch my legs," I said.

"What does that mean?" Meryl asked.

"You know. Go for a walk."

"You?"

"Why not me?"

Meryl put her teacup down on the table. "No reason. It's just that I've never seen you exercise, and the only time I've seen you walk is to get food."

"Let my dolly stretch her legs," Grandma said and winked at me. "Maybe she's training to do the Ironman Triathlon. It's in Hawaii. Go stretch your legs, bubbeleh. You'll be a few steps closer to Hawaii."

I practically ran out of the house and down the driveway. Looking both ways for cars, but more importantly for witnesses, I crossed the street. Once across, I watched for people again, but nobody was out, so I went around the side of Pablo's house, found an unlocked window, and climbed inside.

It was technically a crime, but not really since the owner was dead. At least that's what I would tell the police if they caught me.

The house was in pristine condition. Nothing had been changed, and nothing had been moved out. I wondered if Pablo had had any family, and if the house was going to be sold or if someone else was going to move in.

But for the moment, I didn't care. I was looking for clues.

This case had a sad lack of clues.

First, I searched Pablo's library. I found terrifying credit card bills and an impressive collection of erotic art, but nothing that would explain why he had gotten axed to death.

Then, I moved to his bathroom and checked his medicine cabinet. Pablo had more anxiety medications than a tightrope walker. No wonder he had always seemed so chipper. He was as high as a kite and feeling no pain.

In his bedroom, I checked under his mattress and in his drawers. Nothing. Ditto his studio. I plopped down on the couch in his living room and looked around.

"If I were incriminating evidence, where would I hide?" I asked out loud.

As if to answer, the doorbell rang.

CHAPTER 12

All right, dolly. Let's talk about music. You know, like Elvis. When that man used to sing, it made my body do things. Good things. Music can bring out emotion. And you want the right emotion. Especially from a man. So, pick the music for the groom. The bride is already there just with the flower arrangements, but the groom needs mood music to get him in the right frame of mind. Find the music that gets the man emotional. Remind him that he's in love.

– Lesson 12, Wedding Business Advice From
Your Grandma Zelda

I froze in place. I thought about hiding under the couch, but I couldn't fit. I was going to be arrested for sure, and Spencer wouldn't help me. He would probably throw away the key.

What was I going to do? Where could I hide?

The doorbell rang, again. They obviously knew I was there. I had only one thing I could do. I needed to open the door and lie like the liar I was.

I opened the front door and was surprised that it wasn't the police. It was a stranger. A well-dressed man, carrying a briefcase.

His face dropped in surprise when he saw me. "I'm sorry. I thought this was Pablo Cohen's residence."

"It is."

The man put his hand out, and I shook it. "I'm Franklin Upton. You know, the publisher."

I had no idea who he was. I'd never heard of him.

"Pablo and I have an appointment for him to sign his book contract. We're very excited about it. Finding a skull in a backyard that opens up an investigation into an unsolved murder? That doesn't happen every day."

The skull. I had completely forgotten about the skull.

"You mean the skull of the miner?" I asked.

The publisher laughed. "No, of the missing girl. Pablo's found some tantalizing clues and discovered her identity. He hasn't told us yet, though. Do you know?"

I had stopped listening to him. Instead, my mind was replaying the events before the wedding.

Pablo's pool men had discovered a skull, and

work on the pool had stopped. Still, Pablo was excited about the discovery. So excited that he kept digging on his own?

Had he found something else? Something that revealed the identity of the remains?

There was something I was forgetting. Something important about Pablo. What had he done differently before the wedding?

Oh, yes. Now, I remembered. He had left a note for Spencer. He needed to talk to him. But when Spencer approached Pablo at the wedding, he didn't want to talk, anymore. Why not?

A theory began to build in my mind.

"Did Pablo tell the police about it?" I asked the publisher.

He shook his head. "He's going to tell them after he completes his investigation."

A little bubble of realization popped in my brain. I knew why Pablo had been murdered. It wasn't because he was a jerk. It was because he was nosy.

I clutched at my throat. *Oh, my God. I'm nosy, too.*

"So, he already started investigating?" I asked.

The publisher nodded. "That's why he's getting a high, six-figure book deal."

It all made sense. Finally.

"I'm sorry to inform you that Pablo Cohen is dead," I told the publisher, gently.

"What? I don't believe you."

"Freak accident two days ago." I decided to leave out the gory details. He only needed to push a few buttons on his phone to learn all about it.

"Well, I better be getting home," I said, once the publisher had digested the news and understood that his business here was over. "I live across the street. I'm so sorry for your loss."

That night, time had never moved so slowly. Seconds had turned into minutes. Minutes into hours. And hours just wouldn't pass at all.

I had feigned fatigue early and went up to bed right after dinner. I lay there for who knew how long until I heard Spencer come up and get into bed. I pretended to snore lightly so he wouldn't get any ideas about getting frisky, and finally, he fell asleep.

I waited for an hour after that. Then, I knew he was out. He was sleeping like a stone.

Quietly, I rolled out of bed and tiptoed out of the room. Pablo's house was practically calling to me.

I had been looking for clues this afternoon in his house, but I should have been looking outside.

Bringing a flashlight, I slowly opened the front

door, stepped outside, and closed the door with a soft click. The neighborhood was dead quiet. It looked like everyone was tucked in their beds in their homes. All except for me. I was going to find out what Pablo knew because that's what had gotten him killed.

I padded barefoot across the street and didn't turn my flashlight on until I was in Pablo's backyard. Remembering about the large hole for the pool, I switched the light on and scanned the area. There were huge mounds of dirt everywhere, a large hole for the pool, and work equipment scattered around.

I thought back to exactly where they had discovered the skull. It was easy to find. I laid the flashlight on a nearby mound of dirt and examined the area.

There was nothing sticking out. No more clues. But I got the impression that it had been dug up further since the last time I had seen it. I tried to dig with my hands, but with the dry weather, the earth was hard to move.

I needed a shovel.

I saw the shadow of one sticking up nearby, and I pulled it out of the dirt after a few hard tugs.

"Now, let's see what secrets I can dig up," I said, excited.

I slammed the shovel into the ground and turned

the dirt over. It was hard to dig without using my foot on the shovel, but since I wasn't wearing shoes, I had no choice. After about five minutes of digging, I was thrilled that the shovel hit something hard.

I dropped to my knees and shined the light on the little hole I had made. I didn't see a thing, but when I put my hand inside, I could feel something.

A box?

My pulse began to race. Eureka! I dug around the box with my hands until I finally freed it.

But it wasn't a box. It was a briefcase. Something about it made me scared, and for the first time since sneaking into Pablo's backyard, I had the feeling that someone was watching me.

I shined the light around me, but there was no one.

I returned my attention to the briefcase. It was locked. I knew how to pick locks, but my handy-dandy lock picks were in my purse at home. I would have to take the briefcase with me to see what was inside.

I kept digging in the hole to find more clues. Maybe a leg bone or an arm bone.

Bones.

Bones!

Oh my God. The skull. Where was the skull?

With all of my searching in the house, I hadn't

found the skull.

And that's when I knew that whatever else Pablo had found was hidden away with the skull.

Now that I had the briefcase, I probably didn't need whatever Pablo had found, but since I was sure that whatever he had found was the reason for his murder, I was determined to find it.

Leaving the briefcase on the ground, I stood and shined the light around me. I still couldn't shake the feeling that I was being watched, but I shrugged it off.

"If I were a lecherous artist, where would I hide my treasure?" I asked out loud.

I had already searched in the house. Would Pablo have put the skull back in the ground?

No. He would have wanted access to it.

But where was a safe hiding place outside? I shined my light again, and it fell on the pool filter. Not attached to anything, its basket was sitting by the retaining wall, looking completely out of place.

Could it be that easy? What kind of shmuck hid a skull outside in a basket? I carefully walked around the large hole in the ground to get to the basket. I opened it, but there was nothing inside.

When I went to put it back, I realized that it had been placed against a sturdy, opaque acrylic box, which was nestled in a cubby hole in the retaining wall. The basket must have been used as a sort of marker to remind Pablo where he had hidden the box.

But he was still a shmuck to hide a skull outside in a work zone, as far as I was concerned. I flipped the brackets that were used to seal the box, and I opened it.

Inside, I found the skull in a large Ziploc bag. Carefully, I took it out and searched the box. At first, I thought it was empty, but stuck to the bottom was another—small this time—Ziploc bag.

I held my breath and pulled it out. I shined my light on it and saw that it was an old library card. It belonged to Joni Collins, and there was a black and white picture of her glued to the card, along with her address. She had lived nearby, outside the Historic District in a neighborhood of tiny, one-story cottages.

From her photo, Joni couldn't have been more than eighteen-years-old. I looked down at the skull and knew that it was her.

I also knew that eighteen-year-old girls didn't carry bulky briefcases.

An icy feeling of dread crawled up my spine, and the feeling of being watched hit me strong, again. Quickly, I returned the skull to the box, and I slipped the library card into my pajama pocket.

I turned to go back to the briefcase, but I tripped over some dirt and fell down the large hole for the pool, landing on something hard.

I screamed as I fell, and when I landed at the bottom, I felt for broken bones.

First one leg.

Then, the other.

Then, the third leg.

Then, the fourth.

Hold on a minute.

How many legs did I have?

I counted again. One, two, three, four.

Two were a lot larger than the other two. My flashlight had fallen by my head, and I grabbed it.

"Gladie!" I heard Spencer yell from across the street. Good. He could get me out of the hole.

I shined the light on my legs. Two were wearing pajama pants, and two were wearing fitted, men's slacks. I shined the light up the slacks. Those legs were attached to a body with a face that had been bludgeoned to death.

"Hello, Mr. Publisher," I said. "That must be your briefcase."

And then everything went black.

I swam in inky blackness for a while, trying to get out of it, but I seemed hopeless to succeed. Then, I heard Spencer's voice, yelling at me.

Why was he yelling at me? He was my husband.

He wasn't supposed to yell at me. He was supposed to whisper sweet endearments and give me presents. Like chocolate. I could have gone for some chocolate right about then. And maybe cheesecake. And fried chicken.

Spencer's voice got even louder, and I could finally make out the words he was saying.

"No, no, no, no," he was wailing.

No? I was sick and tired of being told, no. I needed to be free! I needed…What did I need?

"Please God, let her be all right. Gladie, open your eyes. Oh my God, please be okay!"

I felt my body being shaken, and I finally managed to open my eyes. Spencer was in the hole with me, cradling me in his arms.

"Are you crying?" I asked, surprised. "Have I ever seen you cry before?"

"You're alive!" he cried. "Oh my God, you're alive!"

"You sound like Doctor Frankenstein."

"I thought I had lost you. I thought you were gone forever."

"I think I fainted."

"I thought you had been murdered," Spencer said, his voice choked with emotion. "Are you sure you're all right?"

"All four of my legs are fine. But he's not fine.

Really not fine. I think the blood is his. Don't look, Spencer. You'll faint, too."

Spencer held me tighter. "Pinky, didn't I tell you to stay out of trouble?"

"What trouble? Am I in trouble?"

CHAPTER 13

The tender moments between a couple before their wedding are the most important, bubbeleh. It's not the fakakta proposal with the fireworks and the band. No, it's those quiet little moments right before the "I do." Give them the quiet moment. Let them breathe. Let them soak it right in. Then, pounce like a killer party planner and make them do the Bunny Hop. But not until they get their moment.

— Lesson 13, Wedding Business Advice From Your Grandma Zelda

I was being treated like a princess, and I loved it. Since Spencer had carried me home the night before and tenderly bathed me and treated my cuts and scrapes, he had not let me out of his sight.

He had put me to bed with a cup of cocoa and let

me sleep late. When I woke, he was at my bedside looking at me with so much love and concern, that I felt like the richest woman in the world.

He explained that Remington was doing the forensics across the street, and it wasn't until mid-morning that Spencer asked for my rundown on what had exactly happened the night before.

I almost told him the whole truth. I just left out the parts that could get me into trouble, like about breaking into the house. I also held back about the library card and Joni Collins' identity.

I wasn't going to hold back that information forever, though. I just wanted twenty-four hours to investigate on my own. I needed closure. I planned on turning over everything to Spencer tomorrow evening, no matter what.

At ten-thirty in the morning, Spencer helped me downstairs to sit in the parlor, even though I was perfectly capable of walking and sitting on my own. Grandma brought in a tray of bagels, lox, and coffeecake for me, and a few minutes later, Bird entered the house with her pedicurist to take care of Grandma's once-a-week spa day.

They decided to set up in the parlor instead of the kitchen, in order to keep me company. But I also thought that Bird wanted to talk to me. And I was right.

"That crazy boob woman is suing me!" Bird exclaimed and began to put Grandma's hair in rollers. "Can you imagine the nerve of that woman? How dare she? It's bad enough that your husband arrested me and shackled me to the wall," she continued and shot Spencer a dirty look.

He was standing in the parlor's doorway, leaning against the doorjamb with his arms crossed in front of him. He was wearing jeans and a button-down shirt, and he looked good enough to eat, like a hot fudge sundae with one of those long spoons that gets every last drop.

"Shackles might be a slight exaggeration," he said. "And you were never actually arrested, Bird."

Bird pointed a curler at him. "I had to use the police restroom, though. That was bad enough. I have one word for you, Spencer: Bleach."

It turned out that the boob lady was suing Bird for personal assault and mental anguish. To top it all off, the *Hunger Games* lady owner of *Moo!* was also suing Bird because she had damaged her "best milker."

"Gladie, those lunatics are going to ruin me. They're going to take my salon."

"Careful with the curlers, Bird," Grandma said. "You got them wound so tight that my ears are at the back of my head."

"Sorry, Zelda," Bird said. "I'm a tight curler

when I'm emotional."

She pointed another curler at Spencer. "Why don't you arrest that *Moo!* place?" she asked him. "It's disgusting."

"I've been busy hunting an alligator, but I'm sending Margie over there because of a couple complaints."

Bird clutched at her chest. "Thank goodness. And Gladie, you'll be my witness, won't you? You'll say that I was only defending myself?"

I took a bite of my bagel. "I didn't see anything, Bird. I was blind at the time."

"So?" Bird said, her voice rising an octave. "Are we friends or not?"

Grandma squirmed in her seat. "Dolly, tell the judge that the breast milker was abusive, or Bird is going to pull my scalp off with these rollers."

"Sorry again, Zelda," Bird said and started to re-do the rollers at the speed of light. "I've been so stressed. I can't focus." She put a curler down and dipped a popsicle stick in a vat of hot wax. Then, she rounded on me with it. "Here we go," she sang and slathered it on my upper lip, while I was chewing a bite of bagel. Then, a second later, she put a strip of linen on the wax and ripped it off. "Finally. No more mustache. You looking like Magnum PI. No wonder I couldn't concentrate."

Spencer burst out laughing.

My eyes flicked to the grandfather clock. I was itching to visit Joni Collins' address, but Spencer was shadowing me. I liked being treated like a princess, but even Snow White got some alone time in the forest once in a while.

"Don't you have to go to work?" I asked Spencer.

He shook his head. "Nope. I took the day off. I'm with you all day."

I bit my lower lip. "What if the alligator terrorizes the town?"

"If the alligator terrorizes the town, I'll go back to work. What's the matter, Pinky? I get the impression that you want to get rid of me."

"If you were my husband, I'd never get rid of you," the pedicurist said while she scraped my grandmother's heels. "I'd wrap my legs around you and would never let go."

There was a moment of silence in the room, and it took me a minute to remember what I had wanted to say.

"I have a meeting at two o'clock," I told Spencer. "For the Spindle wedding."

It was going to be totally different than the Bass-Chu wedding. Much more low key and with a much tighter budget. I was looking forward to a more relaxing wedding. The bride was sweet and undemanding and thoroughly in love.

I also figured that the meeting would be quick, and I could go over to Joni's address right after.

"I'll go with you," Spencer said.

"To a wedding planning meeting?"

He smirked his little smirk. "Yep."

"We're going to be talking about tulle."

He shrugged. "I don't know what that is, but I think I can handle it."

Spencer signaled to me to come out on the porch with him. I excused myself and joined him there.

"Yes?" I asked.

"I can't handle this," he said.

I put my hands on my hips. "I knew you couldn't."

Spencer was frazzled. We had spent the last hour discussing the bride's mother's insistence that no wedding guest was allowed to pee standing up in their bathroom because that would lead to a lake of urine on the floor that no one would want to clean up.

"This is a terrible way to make a living," Spencer told me. "Those people are crazy."

I shushed him. "Pipe down. They'll hear you.

They're not crazy. They're just particular about their happily ever after. Besides, I was going to buy you Padres season tickets with my paycheck."

"You were?" he asked, surprised. "Pinky, I didn't know you were so romantic."

"Go chase an alligator. I'll call Bridget or Lucy to pick me up."

He kissed me lightly on the lips. "Okay, but don't get into trouble."

I promised, but I crossed my fingers behind my back. I called Lucy, but she didn't pick up. But Bridget did, and she said she would be right over.

When I went back into the house, the bride's mother had the freezer open.

"We'll serve these turkeys for the reception," she announced.

I looked in the freezer. Three turkeys were languishing at the bottom in inches of ice and freezer burn.

"How long have they been in the freezer?" I asked.

"I don't know. I think Clinton was president when I put them in there. Safeway was having a sale, if I remember correctly."

"Is it safe?"

"Is it safe?" She opened the refrigerator and took

out a jar with a glob of something inside it. "I've kept my uterus in the fridge for seven years, and it's just fine. So, I'm sure a turkey in a freezer can last forever."

I rubbed my ears. "I'm sorry. I think I heard you wrong. What's in the jar?"

She tapped the jar and hugged it to her chest. "My uterus. I keep it to show my children where they used to live."

Bridget picked me up in her Volkswagen Bug just after the bride and her mother finally decided that the "No peeing standing up" sign should be bashful pink to match the bridesmaids' dresses.

I couldn't get into Bridget's car fast enough. "Love takes a lot of planning," I told her.

Bridget was wearing all black, again, and her ski mask was stuffed in the drink holder in the center console.

"I told Lucy I was picking you up, and she told me to dress for detective work. She wants to meet us, but I didn't know where we're going," she said.

I called Lucy and gave her the cross-street by Joni's house. So, we could meet a little way away from the house.

"I'm afraid we didn't find out anything at the brunch," Bridget told me on the drive. "Because Lucy walked into some poison oak, and the neighbor's dog came after us, and we had to jump over a hedge. That's when Lucy fell on a mound of doggie doo. Don't tell her I told you. I don't think she wants anyone to know she had doggie doo all over her. She had to strip down before getting in her car, and I had to shield her with my body, but a man stealing avocados saw her and dropped his avocados, and one rolled over to a woman who was breastfeeding her boyfriend."

"That's quite a story," I remarked.

"The woman had quit her job to breastfeed her boyfriend every two hours. They got the idea from *Moo!* but it's been quite time-consuming, and they don't know how long they can keep it going."

"How do you know all this, Bridget?"

She took a deep breath. "I felt bad about the man's avocado because they're so scarce these days, so I went to get it for him, but then I left Lucy naked in the street, so she screamed and jumped into the car. She put the car into neutral before she remembered to turn on the motor, and the car rolled over the avocado and into the breastfeeding couple, breaking two of the man's toes."

I nodded. "I get it. So, you took him to the hospital and found out about the breastfeeding."

"No. When the car ran into him, that's when I noticed what he was doing. I projectile vomited, just like little Jonathan did when I took him to the San Diego Fair and let him eat three funnel cakes. The vomit went all over the couple, but I slipped on it and bumped my head. The man with the broken toes took me to the hospital for a concussion protocol, and he told me all about it in the car."

She took a deep breath, like it was all she could do to get that story out.

"Well…" I said and drifted off. It took me a full minute to figure out what to say. "How's your head?"

"Fine. But the guy had to get a cast."

I nodded. "Don't worry about Lucy. I won't say a thing about the doggie doo. I'm only half-sure that she actually poops in the first place, so I can imagine how traumatic her dog poop encounter was."

We met Lucy at the corner near Joni's house, and I told my friends everything that had happened the night before and everything that I had learned.

"Look at you, darlin'. You're tripping over dead people, again. It's just like the good old days."

"No, I tripped over some dirt, and I *fell* on a dead person."

Lucy snapped her fingers. "That's right. You're usually a faller, not a tripper." She slipped her ski mask on. "So, what're we doing? I brought a stun gun and a pair of brass knuckles."

"Well, this girl has been missing for over fifty years, so maybe let's just talk to her family instead of going Rambo on their asses," I suggested.

"Right. Of course, you're right," Lucy said, sounding disappointed. "I just got so excited. There's a killer out there, axing folks and beating them to death and throwing them into pools. Just thinking about it gets my blood racing."

I felt her pain. My blood was doing the same thing.

"The killer might have been a troubled youth who fell through the cracks and tumbled into a heartless and inept justice system," Bridget theorized.

"Or he's a no-good psychopath who doesn't deserve a moment's compassion, darlin'," Lucy offered. "Like Charlie Manson. Nobody's shedding a tear over Manson's childhood, and for good reason."

"I think we may be losing focus," I said. "I'm going to visit Joni's family, and I'll be right back. They might get scared if they see a couple ninjas, so you two hold back here for now."

Bridget and Lucy agreed. I walked the half a block to the address on the library card and was surprised and disappointed to find it boarded up. It had boarded for a long time because the boards were covered in graffiti in a town with no graffiti, and the lawn looked like it had been forgotten decades ago.

I went back to Bridget and Lucy and gave them the update.

"We need to break into that house," Bridget said. "We can't leave the trail cold."

I sighed. I had had enough of breaking into houses, but I knew she was right.

"Good. I'll get my crowbar," Lucy said.

Lucy and Bridget went around to the back of the house to pry a board loose, while I went to the front porch to look around. I felt like Scout on Boo Radley's porch. It was both scary and filled with wonder. Where had the family gone? Did they die of grief over their missing daughter? Did they move away because they couldn't bear being in the town that took their daughter away from them? And why didn't they sell their house? Why was it still standing here, unused and neglected?

I tried the mailbox, but it had been nailed shut. I went to test the front door, but I stopped when I noticed that part of the door handle had been wiped clean where someone had recently touched it.

Instantly, I knew that it had been Pablo. He had been right there on the porch where I was standing. I turned around, looking to see what he had seen.

What had Pablo done here, exactly? But I knew. He had skulked. This was where the skateboarders must have seen Pablo skulking. Right here in this neighborhood.

Who else had seen him skulking? And was that what had gotten him killed?

But nobody was out now, and nobody was there to take notice of me. The neighborhood was quiet and clean, and it looked like everyone minded their own business.

I went around back, just as Bridget and Lucy managed to pry a board off of a window. We all peeked through it.

"Totally empty. Totally abandoned," Lucy said, disappointed.

We had run up against another dead end. We put the board back as best as we could, and we returned to the front of the house. Just as we reached the sidewalk, I saw Debbie's catering van pull away and drive up the street.

"That's a helluva coincidence," I said, watching the van drive away.

"Oh my goodness, I was right," Lucy breathed. "The caterers are always guilty."

"We don't know that," I said. "It could be a coincidence. It might not have even been her van."

"It was her van," Bridget said. "I recognized the license plate. I'm a bookkeeper. I have an eye for numbers."

CHAPTER 14

Sometimes you got to take one for the team, dolly. Love is about partnerships, not solo trips around the world. You get what I'm saying? I don't want to be schmaltzy, but if you love someone, you'll do anything, even make a fool of yourself. You can't focus on the humiliations when you just want to keep love alive. And you need to bring that attitude into your weddings, bubbeleh. Don't worry if you're humiliated wearing the hot pink, floor-length dress. It's all part of the love game.

— Lesson 14, Wedding Business Advice From
Your Grandma Zelda

Bridget and Lucy decided to stake out the boarded house in case Debbie's van came back. Lucy stayed behind, while Bridget drove me home, and then she was going to stop at Saladz to stock up on stakeout meals for them.

While they were staking out the neighborhood, I had other ideas. I was going to go to the best information resource our town had.

I was going to talk to the blue-haired librarian.

Cannes had only one library, and it was the kind of library that had nonstop business. The checkout line was always long. There was always a slew of men working on their World War Two books. There was always a story-time circle happening for children. And the computers were always full of people using the internet.

Meryl was in charge of the entire operation. The library was in an Old Western style building with a fake two-story front. But it was really only one-story and about two thousand square feet.

Meryl was very proud that she kept a large collection in such a tight space. She had one librarian for children's books, one librarian for adult fiction, and Meryl herself was all about the research materials.

After Bridget dropped me off at home, I got in my car without going into the house first. Spencer's car was in the driveway, and I wanted to sneak out without him. He had been sweet and attentive after the pool incident, but I also knew that he wanted to keep tabs on me and prevent me from getting involved in the murder.

Of course, I couldn't let that happen.

Duh.

Across the street, Remington had cordoned off the entire house. As I opened my car door, I saw him come out of the house carrying his large forensics case. He must have worked all night and this morning. He waved at me, and I waved back. Then, I got into my car and drove to the library.

I got an electric shock when I went to open the library door, and I cursed the dry weather. My skin was so dry and cracked from the weather that I wished someone would slather me in Crisco again.

Walking inside the library, I was instantly more relaxed. It was quiet and temperature-controlled, and there was an air of the soothing assurance that books promised. So much more relaxing than a Netflix binge.

Even though there were quite a few people there, they all kept to themselves, quietly reading, writing, researching, or searching for books. Even the kids were being well-behaved and quiet.

I stood in line to talk to Meryl. The three people before me asked her questions, and she dispatched them easily.

"Can we talk somewhere a little private?" I whispered.

She signaled silently at me to follow her. We

walked to a small utility room in the back. It was more like a large supply closet, but it also served as a staff room with cubbies for their belongings, a table, and four chairs.

Once we were inside, Meryl closed the door.

"What's up?" she asked and opened the fridge. She took out two child-sized chocolate milk boxes, handed me one, and took a seat at the table.

I sat across from her, popped the little straw into my milk box, and took a sip. Then, I took the Ziploc bag with Joni's library card out of my purse and slid it over to Meryl.

"What's this?" she asked, opening the bag. Her face brightened when she saw it. "They don't make cards like this these days. Look at the work they put into it. The typing. Gluing the picture on so carefully. And they put her address on it." She looked up from the card. "How did you get this?"

"I found it." It wasn't a lie. I had found it when I was illegally trespassing.

"What a crazy coincidence."

I sat up straight in my chair. "What? What's a coincidence?"

"Pablo Cohen came in here with the same library card. When was that?" she asked like she was talking to herself.

"The day before he was killed," I supplied.

She pointed at me and nodded. "Yes. The day before he died. He asked for our records on our library cardholders. I explained we didn't have records that went back that far. This card must go back to the seventies."

"The sixties."

Meryl's face brightened, again. "The sixties. Oh, I would love for us to have this. I would frame it and put it on the checkout desk."

"Maybe later," I told her. "Did Pablo ask you to research the cardholder by name? You know, in Cannes' historical documents?"

"No. He just asked for our records on cardholders. We don't keep that sort of thing, anyway. That's national library database stuff. We're an email-address-only operation these days. Sad, really."

"Do you recognize the girl? How about her name?"

Meryl adjusted her glasses and studied the card. "Not the girl, but maybe her name. She's a local girl according to the address."

I took a deep breath. "Meryl, what I'm about to tell you, you need to keep under your hat for at least a day."

Meryl smiled and rubbed her forearms. "Oh, Gladie. You just gave me goosebumps. You sounded so serious. I guess we're not talking about weddings here."

I leaned over the table and tapped the card, which she was still holding. "I think Joni Collins went missing decades ago, and I think that Pablo discovered her skull and this card in his backyard."

Meryl stared at me, wide-eyed. "What was she doing there?" Then, it dawned on her. "She was murdered there, Gladie? Is this one of your cases?"

I nodded. "I think she was murdered, and her body was hidden there. Hidden when they built the pool. And I think Pablo was murdered because he found the card."

Meryl studied the library card, again. "Holy smokes. This is just like a Hitchcock film. Wait a second. Did you come here to get my help?"

I was worried that she was getting scared and wouldn't help me, so I tried to come up with a lie.

"Well…"

"Oh!" Meryl cried. "You did! I've always wanted to be Miss Marple. You know, I've read every single Agatha Christie and PD James. Twice. Whatever you want me to do, I'm on it. What do you want me to do?"

I wanted her to work her research magic. I left her the card and set her loose to find out everything she could about Joni Collins, her house, and the cursed house across the street where they found her skull.

Meryl promised to get right to work on it and

saluted me when I left.

On my way out of the library, I called Bridget to find out how the stakeout was going. She said they had eaten lunch, and there had been no movement at the house and no sign of the van. They were going to sit around for two more hours before they had to pick up their kids.

I put a layer of Chapstick on my lips, slung my purse over my shoulder, and walked to my car. I had parked in the furthest spot by the exit, and as I got nearer, I noticed that a couple kids were standing around it, putting something on the roof.

"Hey, you kids!" I called. "What're you doing? Stop that!"

They ran away for a short distance but stopped, turned around, and started pointing and laughing at me.

I squinted, unsure that I recognized them. But then I was sure. Yes, I did recognize them. The last time I had seen them, they had thrown a sex sheep at me.

Oh no.

I turned back around to check on my car. The teenagers had put a sex doll on the roof of it. Where the hell did they get another sex doll? Did they have a warehouse of them at home?

"Very funny," I called after them. "Very mature. Your mother must be so proud."

They laughed loudly at that comment.

I went to take the sex doll off of my car, but it was stuck. I tugged and tugged, but it wouldn't budge. The juvenile delinquents were laughing hysterically.

"You *glued* a sex doll to the roof of my car?" I shrieked at them, which made them laugh even louder.

They must have used professional-grade glue because no matter what I did, I couldn't budge it. The sex doll was lying on its back with its legs facing forward and wide open to show the world its highly realistic anatomy. I moved around the car to the driver's side, trying to pull the doll off, but I had no luck.

They had dropped a sex sheep on the ground by the driver's door, probably because they didn't have enough time to glue it to the car like they did with the doll. It was like they had a collection of these things or something. I picked it up to throw it at the obnoxious teenagers, who were still laughing at their prank.

I lifted the sheep over my head to get a good throw, but when I tried to toss it, I realized that it was stuck to my head.

I hadn't realized that the damned kids had put glue on the sheep. And now, I had managed to stick it to my head.

"She's got a sheep stuck to her head!" one of the teenagers cried, and they all burst into side-splitting hysterics.

"What on earth do you have on your head? Is that a new style?" Ruth asked me when I walked into Tea Time.

I slapped my Robinson Bucks card on the bar. "Ruth, I want a pumpkin spice latte, extra foam, extra everything, and a few pumps of caramel. Then, I want a piece of cake."

"What kind of cake?"

"Every kind of cake. I want a piece of every kind of cake that you have."

Ruth wiped the bar with a rag. "Pumpkin spice is a seasonal thing. I don't serve it in August."

I grabbed hold of Ruth's shirt and pulled her close. "Ruth," I whispered, like Dirty Harry. "If I don't get pumpkin spice pumping through my veins, I can't be responsible for the damage I'll do."

She blinked and slid a slice of chocolate cake over to me and handed me a fork. "I'll give you the pumpkin spice if you tell me what's on your head."

"The two front legs of a sex sheep. There. Are you happy? Now, you know."

Ruth started to make the coffee. "I've been thinking about this whole bomb cyclone of weirdness we're in," she mused. "and I think it was brought in by the sickos next door. I mean, what are the babies in this country going to do if all of the breast milk is going to depraved individuals? And how about those women's breasts? If they keep breastfeeding every Tom, Dick, and Harry, they're going to have old lady's breasts like mine, and that's just not right at their age."

She handed me the latte, and I took a big sip, letting the sugar and caffeine try to heal me from within. Ruth couldn't stop staring at my head.

"It used to be a whole sex sheep, but Meryl managed to cut most of it off with the library's paper cutter," I explained.

"Uh-huh," Ruth said, still staring at my head.

"Yes, we tried nail polish remover and Goo Gone. The teenagers must have used some kind of NASA glue or something. You know, some kind of glue to keep spaceships intact if they're hit by a meteor shower."

There was the sound of brakes squealing and then a loud crash outside, along with the sound of metal on metal in a huge impact.

"What on earth?" Ruth said.

I dug into the chocolate cake. "It's probably just another car crash."

"*Another*? How many have there been today?"

"Three on my way over here. I guess the anatomically correct hoo-ha coming at oncoming traffic distracts drivers and *pow!*, they crash."

Ruth put her hand on my forehead. "Are you all right, girl? Not coming down with something? Like malaria or paranoid schizophrenia?"

The door opened, and a man ran in, holding a steering wheel.

"The horror!" he shouted. "The horror! There's a woman trapped on a car! A naked woman! And you can see *everything.*"

I arched an eyebrow at Ruth. "See? It has an impact on people. Have you seen Bird around? Her salon is closed today, but I was hoping she could get the sheep legs off of my head. Otherwise, I'm going to have to shave it."

Ruth put her hand on my forehead, again. "No fever," she noted, like she didn't quite believe it. "Maybe I was wrong about *Moo!* being the cause of the weirdness bomb cyclone. Maybe something else caused it. Or *someone* else."

I ate half of the chocolate cake and drank two lattes, and when I finally felt sedated, I left Tea Time to find Bird. On my way out the door, Lou came in. He was staring at my head.

"It's a sex sheep's legs, Lou," I told him, and he walked into a wall.

Outside, two cars had had a head-on collision

near my car, and the drivers were exchanging driver's licenses in the middle of the street. Luckily, they must have slowed down to a crawl to see the sex doll on my roof when they crashed, so nobody was hurt, and the cars only suffered fender damage.

A crowd of people were standing around my car, trying to save the woman glued to the roof. As I passed, a couple of them figured out that the woman wasn't real, and then they started to comment on the pervert who owned the car.

Ruth had told me that Bird had been seen stalking *Moo!*, so I went next door.

I had never gone inside the new shop before, and it was pretty much the way I expected.

Only worse.

CHAPTER 15

You ever get the feeling that everything is going to plan, Dolly? You ever feel that you're near the end, that closure is around the corner, and that a happy ending is imminent? Well, forget about it! As a wedding planner, you need to be vigilant until the couple is away on their honeymoon. Stay alert. Don't be a putz.

— Lesson 15, Wedding Business Advice From Your Grandma Zelda

Moo! was a wonder of clean, modern design, all white with only a splash of light blue. Light blue boobs, mostly. Pictures of light blue boobs on the walls. A chrome sculpture of boobs by the door. A boob mural by the cash register.

All the boobs are enormous, full and unnaturally

round and perky.

The word "bosoms" kept replaying in my mind because that's what they were. Big, comfy bosoms, the kind that men dream about nestling in for comfort.

I felt like throwing up.

A giant plastic stork hung from the ceiling, carrying a baby bottle in its beak. There was a milk bar to the right that looked like an old-fashioned ice cream counter with twelve stools. Nearly all of the stools were occupied.

Every single customer was male, except for me. And every staff member was female with enormous bosoms. There was the female cashier, the woman manning the milk bar, and a woman walking around with a white, circular platter, offering free samples.

"Would you like to try a shot of our finest Superfood Mammary Antioxidant Power Boost?" she asked me. Her eyes flicked to my head for the briefest moment and then returned to my eyes.

Smooth.

That's what I called good customer service. Never stare at a woman's sex sheep legs. I was pretty sure that was in a service manual somewhere.

I glanced at the tiny paper cups filled with white liquid that she was offering. Blech.

"No, thank you," I said. "I'm just looking for

someone."

Bird wasn't in the store, but Mayor Robinson was sitting on the stool at the end of the milk bar. He was sipping something out of a large white cup, and he had a milk mustache. There was a Band-Aid wrapped around each of his fingers. We locked eyes for a second, and then he averted his eyes, looking around, like he was searching for an exit.

I sat down on the stool next to him. "Hello, Mr. Mayor." He looked at my head, and his mouth dropped open, but I guess he couldn't think of words to say. "It's a hat. Lady Gaga has the same one."

He kept staring at it. In fact, he had stopped blinking entirely and was just fixed on it. "Who's Lady Gaga?" he asked. "Is that one of the queen's daughters?"

"I'm looking for Bird," I told him, changing the subject. "Have you seen her around here?"

"She was here a minute ago. She was wearing a hat, too. I think she went in the back room through the 'staff only' door."

I started to get up, but he stopped me. "Hold on. I want to give you the new Robinson Bucks card. There was a little dust-up around the first batch of cards, so I made improvements."

He put a plastic card on the counter in front of me. It looked like the other Robinson Bucks card, but this one was made of plastic, and the picture and writing on it were shiny and in 3-D.

"Cool," I said and picked it up. I felt a sharp pain in two of my fingers, and I dropped the card back on the counter. I inspected my fingers, which were now bleeding.

"That's the one hiccough," the mayor explained, sadly. "The cards are a little sharp. But I'm sure that will wear off in time."

He gave me two Band-Aids from a box of them that he had in his pocket, and I wrapped my fingers. Then, I took a napkin and used it to gingerly pick up the card and place it in my back pocket.

"Maybe you should get the cards remade," I suggested. "You don't want anyone cutting an artery."

"Not you, too. Why does everyone find fault with my Robinson Bucks? They're a genius idea. If we didn't have them, we would have to use dollars and Visa cards. No good can come from that. Remember the chicken in the pharmacy?"

How could I forget? I mean, I had gotten my head caught in a blood pressure cuff.

"Anyway, the town can't afford to make another batch of cards," he explained. The money business is expensive. Take it from me. Hey, is that a new style of eye makeup, too?" he asked. "Is that a royal family fashion like your hat?"

Poor Mayor Robinson. His heart was in a good place, but he was dumber than dirt.

"No," I told him. "That's breast milk."

I got up and walked straight to the door at the back of the store marked, "staff only." Nobody stopped me.

I found Bird spying on *Moo!*'s computer in a small office. She was in disguise in a man's pin-striped suit and a fedora.

"You're so going to get in trouble," I told her.

She shushed me. "I've almost cracked their password. Then, I'll print out everything and use it against them in court."

I nodded, as if that sounded perfectly reasonable and feasible.

"Bird, I have a sex sheep's legs glued to my head with some kind of NASA spaceship glue. Can you get it out of my hair for me?"

She typed furiously on the computer. "Sure. Come to the salon tomorrow, and I'll get it out."

"Tomorrow?" I asked, panicked. "Tomorrow is a long time to wait with a sex sheep's legs stuck to my head."

But she wasn't listening to me, anymore. She was typing fast, not even blinking, like a dog with a stolen bone. I didn't blame her. Her business was in jeopardy, and she was desperate.

I left *Moo!* no better off than when I went in. I could only imagine what Spencer was going to say when he saw me. He would never let me live it down. He would insist that somehow, getting a sex sheep glued to my head was my fault.

Geez, marriage was hard.

Outside, there was still a big crowd gathered around my car. I had hoped that with all of their well-meaning curiosity, one of them would have managed to pry the sex doll off the roof of my car.

Alas, it was still there.

I pushed my way to the car door and unlocked it. Just as I was about to get in, I saw Spencer run down the street carrying a huge net.

"Out of my way!" he shouted. "Run for your life!"

He waved the net around to punctuate his warnings, and he ran incredibly fast in a suit. Fast like his life depended on it.

Around my car, there were murmurs about the alligator in the crowd, and they finally dispersed. I supposed that they were more scared of getting eaten by an alligator than they were curious about a sex doll on a car roof.

Since I hadn't heard from Bridget or Lucy, I

assumed that their stakeout had been a bust. I only hoped that neither of them had wound up in the hospital or covered in excrement again.

Now, it was up to me to run down our last clue. I drove to Debbie's house.

Her van was parked in her driveway, and her garage was open. She was busy folding linens and placing them neatly in marked bins.

She waved at me when she saw me, and then she stopped and stumbled backward.

"What the hell?" she said, looking at my head.

"It's a long story. Bird is going to fix it tomorrow, if she's not in jail for hacking. It's okay if you can't stop staring at it."

She couldn't stop staring at it.

"I'm sorry to bother you again, Debbie," I said. "I needed to talk to you about something."

"That sounds serious," she said, leaning back against one of her dryers.

"Maybe not." I gave her Joni's street address and asked her if she had gone there today.

"235? No."

"Oh." Disappointment washed over me. "I could have sworn it was your van."

"I was at 237, picking up Colin, though."

Colin? Colin lived at 237?

I swear I heard angels singing.

"Colin? Colin lives next door to 235?"

"His whole life, I think. It was his parents' house," she explained.

"Do you have a glass of water? I'm feeling a little light-headed."

She looked at my head and giggled at the light-headed remark. Then, I followed her into her house and sat at the kitchen table. She handed me a glass of ice water.

"Have you known Colin a long time?" I asked her.

"Not really. I had seen him around before he started working for me. He's a jack of all trades, you know. He's a great server. Attentive but unobtrusive. And he likes to work. Like with our last wedding, he called me and asked to work it. You don't see that kind of proactive attitude in this business."

I took a sip of water and tried to think clearly. "You mean he volunteered? When did he do that?"

"That's the thing. It was the night before. Somehow, he knew that we needed more manpower, and he came to the rescue."

He had volunteered the night before the wedding? My suspicious nature was working on overdrive.

"Have you ever heard of Joni Collins?" I asked, taking a shot in the dark. "She lived in the boarded-up house next to Colin in the sixties."

Debbie took a seat across from me. "That house is spooky. It creeps me out every time I see it. Who's Joni Collins?"

"She was a teenager, who disappeared in the sixties."

Debbie's eyes lit up. "Was she one of the girls who disappeared in 1968?"

I stopped breathing. I actually couldn't take a breath.

"There were missing girls?" I managed, finally.

"My mother has talked about it all the time. I guess it didn't get loads of news coverage, though. It was before those kinds of cases made a lot of noise."

"What kinds of cases?" I asked.

"Well, at first a couple girls ran away," Debbie continued. "But then one girl ran away, and nobody thought she would have ever run away because she was a straight-A student. Always at the library. You know, that sort of thing."

My ears perked up. "Always at the library?"

Debbie shrugged. "That's what my mother told me. They were the same age."

My brain was working overtime. Girls that ran

away but maybe didn't run away. It wasn't suspicious enough for the authorities or the media to get involved with, back in those days.

"How many other girls disappeared?" I asked.

"I think one more."

I found myself staring into space, deep in thought about the events that had led up to the wedding:

The skull discovery. The note. The library card. The publishing deal. Volunteering to work the wedding. The murder. And then after the wedding, another murder.

There was something missing in the timeline. Something that would tie it up all with a shiny bow. Something that would give me a definitive answer.

"How old is Colin?" I asked.

"About my mom's age. You want to stay for dinner? I'm serving leftover finger foods from a bar mitzvah I catered a week ago."

Since I didn't want to go home yet and have the sex sheep conversation with Spencer, I accepted the invitation.

Besides, I loved finger foods, and bar mitzvah finger foods, especially. Debbie had made her own delicious version of Bagel Bites in three varieties, fish stick samplers, and spaceship mini pecan pies that were to die for.

I had called Spencer to let him know that I was going to be late, but he didn't answer, so I left a message. "He must be hunting the alligator," I told Debbie.

It was a relief but it only delayed the inevitable. Spencer wanted me to stay out of trouble, but I had managed to get my head Criscoed, my eyeballs milked, my hair burned off, fallen in a pit with a dead body, had a sex sheep stuck to my head, and a life-sized sex doll glued to the roof of my car, which had caused multiple car crashes.

I was happy for Debbie's non-judgmental company and her delicious, nutritionless finger foods.

After dinner, I helped clean up. My Band-Aids got wet, and Debbie gave me a couple new ones to wrap around the fingers that had been cut by the fancy new Robinson Bucks card.

When I went to throw away the Band-Aid wrappers, my phone rang. It was Meryl.

"I found what you're looking for," she said.

"Speak up," I urged. "I can barely hear you."

She said something, but I couldn't hear. "Just come to the library," Meryl yelled into the phone and hung up.

I thanked Debbie for dinner and the information. I got in my car and drove toward the library. Two oncoming cars swerved when their drivers saw me, and they ran onto the sidewalk. They seemed fine, so I just waved at them and kept driving.

It was a good thing it was sunset. Once it was totally dark, nobody would be able to make out the scarily real naked woman on my roof, and I wouldn't be responsible for car crashes around town.

I wondered if I was ever going to be able to get the sex doll off my roof. Maybe it would be stuck there forever. On the bright side, I would always be able to find my car in a crowded parking lot.

Also, maybe I would be able to rent my car out for sexual education classes or bachelor parties.

On the other hand, I was supposed to be a professional. An entrepreneur with my own business. I was supposed to organize tasteful weddings. Be a critical part in a holy communion.

I wondered what my clients would think of the holy communion on the roof of my car.

But maybe Bird would be able to get the sex doll off my car by using the same stuff she was going to use to get the sex sheep's legs off of my head.

But what if she couldn't get it off my head? Maybe she just said that to get rid of me so that she could steal *MOO!*'s company information without me bothering her. Maybe Bird was going to have to shave my head, after all.

My anxiety grew and grew, while I played all of the doomsday scenarios in my mind. By the time I arrived at the library, I was fit to be tied. I parked and got out of the car. I tried once again to pull the sex doll off my car, but it was glued solidly in place.

I gave up and walked to the library's front door. The library was officially closed, but the lights were still on, and Meryl opened the door when I knocked.

I had never seen Meryl so excited. She hopped up and down on her heels while she talked to me.

"I've got so much information for you, Gladie. I feel just like James Bond. Oh, I guess you couldn't get the legs off you," she said, as if she had just noticed my head.

"No," I said, sadly.

"Don't worry. It's hardly noticeable."

Meryl was sweet, but she was a lousy liar.

"What did you find out?" I asked.

"Oh, Gladie, I've got everything. I even have the list of workers on the cursed house's pool in 1968."

My mood lifted from dark doom to euphoria.

"That's wonderful, Meryl."

"Let's sit in the resource stacks, and I'll give you the rundown."

We got halfway there when the light went out.

"Oh, shit," I said.

CHAPTER 16

Exit. Stage right. Or stage left. Sometimes, it's time to call the whole thing off. All the effort, all of the planning. They just don't work. And that's because the foundation doesn't work. Usually, it means that the couple wasn't matched by your Grandma, and so they're not a good fit, and they shouldn't get married in the first place. But the caterer has been booked, and the flowers have been paid for, so they don't want to cancel their wedding. Cancel, dolly! Cancel everything and start fresh. Tell them it's not a loss. It's a new beginning. Believe me, it's not over until the fat lady sings and Elvis leaves the building, and the curtain goes down. Not until all three things happen at once. Only then is it over.

– Lesson 16, Wedding Business Advice From
Your Grandma Zelda

"We should hide," I told Meryl in a whisper.

"It's just the breakers. They blow when we use the electric tea kettle with the microwave."

"Meryl, nobody's using the electric tea kettle with the microwave. The library's closed. We're investigating a murder."

Meryl's mouth dropped open. "We should hide. C'mon."

She took my hand, and we wove between the book stacks until we got to a small table in a dark corner. We dropped to our knees and crawled underneath. There was definitely someone else in the library. We could hear the soft footsteps on the library's thin carpet. Someone had broken in, and he was looking for us.

"Quick," I urged her. "Tell me what you discovered."

"Okay," she whispered. "The cursed house was built in 1968, and they built the pool at the same time. Most of the pool workers are dead. All except two. One of the men who's still living was the actual contractor, and he kept records. It took him a while to look through them in his garage, but he found them. Colin Bacon was one of them, and guess where Colin Bacon lives?"

"He lives next to Joni Collins' house. And he also worked as a waiter at the wedding and was in the tent when Pablo was killed."

Meryl gasped, and I put my hand over her mouth to quiet her so she wouldn't give up our whereabouts to whoever was in the library. She nodded, and I let her go.

"That's not all," she continued. "In 1968, the same year that the pool was built, twelve girls went missing."

"Twelve? I thought it was four."

"Four in Cannes, and another eight in the neighboring towns. They were all the same age, and I don't think they decided to move away together, if you catch my drift."

"You know what this means, Meryl?" I asked and then answered my own question. "It means that Colin Bacon is a serial killer."

"Holy crap. A serial killer in our town? A real one?"

"It's the only thing I can think of. The only thing that makes sense."

"There's one more thing, Gladie. Something you should definitely know," Meryl started, but then there was a noise nearby, and she clamped her mouth closed.

We stared into the darkness from under the table as the sound of soft footsteps came closer. I looked around for a weapon and remembered my purse. I could swing it at Colin and knock him out. It was as good a plan as any.

Suddenly, my phone began to ring, and the noise cut through the quiet library, giving the intruder a beacon call to his victims. The lights came on, and I saw a pair of legs in front of us.

I grabbed my purse and tried to crawl out from under the table. But the sheep's legs got caught on the table and my head was snapped back. That's when I saw that the legs belonged to Colin. And Colin was holding an axe. He had either taken one from the wedding, or he had grown fond of the whole axing idea and bought himself one.

However he armed himself, the serial killer had found us, and we were goners.

"We promise not to talk," I told him.

He laughed at that. Smart guy. He knew a liar when he saw one.

I knew that nothing I could say would stop him. He was simply covering his tracks. Everything that had happened in the past few days was about Colin covering his tracks.

"You had a good run in 1968," I told him. "Nobody ever found the bodies. But then Pablo did, and then what happened?" I asked. He didn't answer, but he didn't have to. "He found the library card. I wondered how you could know about it, but then I realized that you had actually seen it. What had happened, Colin? Pablo went to Joni's house, and you saw him from next door. He stood on the porch, and he must have double-checked the address on the library card."

Colin stared at me blankly, as if I wasn't making any sense, but I knew I was right on target.

"That's when you understood that you had missed something in 1968, and now an arrogant painter was going to be the end of you," I continued. "The thing in the timeline I was missing was what happened next, but that's easy to figure out, too. You went to his house and searched it."

"You're good, Gladie," Meryl whispered.

"You're meticulous, so you kept it nice and neat, but you didn't find anything," I continued. "All you found was the invitation to the wedding, and that was like a gift from the heavens. If you couldn't find the library card, you could at least get rid of Pablo. You called Debbie and offered to work the next day, something unheard of in the business. When the tent collapsed, you took advantage of the moment. That was smart. You took advantage of the confusion. Everybody pointed the finger at everyone else so nobody was really a suspect in the end."

Colin gripped the axe tighter, and I could sense that he was planning his aim. I needed to think of an escape quick.

"But you couldn't leave it at that," I said. "There was still the library card. So, you went back to Pablo's house, but this time, there was somebody there. A publisher. And that publisher was a smart man. He probably guessed who you were. The killer always returns to the scene of the crime...that's something a publisher would think about. And so, you killed him, too."

"Wow, this is just like an Agatha Christie," Meryl whispered. "Go on, Gladie."

"That's it. That's all I got," I said.

I waited for Colin to say something. Usually, at this point in my big Hercule Poirot reveal scene, the killer usually confessed and said something crazy. But Colin was completely quiet. Completely still.

His crazy was the calm, eerie kind of crazy.

The craziest kind of crazy.

"Uh-oh," I said.

I wanted to tell Meryl to run, but I doubted she was very fast and doubted that she could outrun Colin. But maybe I could distract him and give Meryl enough time to run away. How could I signal to her to do that?

There wasn't enough time to devise a plan. Without uttering a sound, he raised his axe. Oh my God. I didn't want to die like this. I didn't want to be axed in the head. I wanted to die when I was one-hundred-and-five in my sleep after a steak dinner at Ruth's Chris. Was that so much to ask?

I shut my eyes tight because I didn't want to see the attack coming.

Somebody screamed.

It wasn't me.

I opened my eyes. My best friend Bridget Donovan, dressed in her ninja outfit, ran at Colin with her sandwich board raised high above her head. She screamed like a woman possessed, hell-bent on sandwich-boarding a serial killer into submission and saving her friend and librarian.

Colin turned around just in time, and Bridget paused, probably because she figured out that an axe was far more lethal than a sandwich board. It looked like we were all doomed.

Suddenly, like a miracle, Colin dropped the axe and grew completely rigid.

Lucy appeared, holding her Taser. The wires had shot out and embedded themselves into Colin. He fell to the floor.

"Look at that, darlin', I *finally* got to use my Taser. Can I use my brass knuckles, too, or is it unsportsmanly to punch a man in the face when he's unconscious?"

I helped Meryl get up, and the four of us hugged

each other and jumped up and down in celebration. We had felled a serial killer. We were going to be town heroes. They were going to name streets after us and give us a parade.

We ran down on the possibilities of hero worship we were going to enjoy for catching a serial killer. They were all wonderful.

"How did you find us?" I asked Bridget and Lucy.

"We've been following the van all day," Bridget explained.

"We're just like the *The Rockford Files*," Lucy said. "We never give up. We sat on that van all day and night. We saw you go visit Debbie, but we just kept watching. We never revealed ourselves."

"Debbie? Then, how did you know I'm here. Debbie's not here," I said.

"She's not?" Bridget asked. "Her van is parked in the parking lot."

As if on cue, Debbie stepped out of the fiction stacks with a gun pointed right at us.

"Oh no," Meryl said. "That's the other thing I wanted to tell you."

"What?" I asked. "What was the other thing you wanted to tell me?"

"Colin is Debbie's uncle. His family house was her family house. Her mother was Colin's twin sister,"

Meryl explained.

"Wow," I said. "Timing is everything. Just think if you had told me that thirty minutes ago."

"You couldn't hear me on the phone," Meryl reminded me. "I would have told you before you got here."

"I'm going to tell Spencer to change our cellphone provider," I grumbled.

Debbie didn't shoot us in the library. She decided to shoot us up in the mountains where no one would find us for a while. When Colin roused, they tied us up with rope from Debbie's van and stuffed us in the trunk of my Oldsmobile Cutlass Supreme. We tried screaming, but I guessed everyone was at home watching television, because nobody came to our rescue.

My trunk was large, but it was hardly big enough for four people. As we were driven away, out of town and up further into the mountains, we tried first to not smother each other.

"Are you happy to see me, or is that a sex sheep glued to your head?" Lucy asked. "It's poking me something awful."

I tried to move away from her, but there wasn't anywhere I could go.

"Ow!" Meryl complained. "You shocked me."

"That's the weather," Bridget said. "Very dry. I'm going to protest the environment when my new sandwich board arrives."

"I don't get shocked," Lucy insisted. "I take supplements to keep me lubricated. Ow!"

"See? You got shocked," Meryl said.

"No, I didn't. That was Gladie's sex sheep again."

"We heard your big speech, Gladie," Bridget told me. "It was very impressive. You sounded just like Columbo."

"I agree," Lucy said. "You were amazing how you wound all of that together. Too bad you had the wrong killer."

But I didn't think I had the wrong killer. Not really. "Colin really is a serial killer," I told them. "He killed those girls in the sixties. And he saw Pablo fishing around Joni's house with the library card. But he must have told his niece Debbie, and for some reason, she took matters in her own hands."

"Because Debbie's parents died when she was little. Colin actually raised her," Meryl said. "I forgot to tell you that, too. Oops."

"This is just like *Criminal Minds*," Lucy said. "The serial killer groomed the girl, and then she became the killer."

That sounded about right. "She killed Pablo, and

she killed the publisher," I said. "I would bet money on it."

"I wonder if she'll let us ask her before she kills us," Bridged mused.

"I'm not letting her kill me," Lucy insisted. "I have things to do. I have a Botox appointment on Wednesday. And no way am I letting Harry raise my triplets on his own. Let's find a weapon in this trunk to get us free from these damned ropes."

"Gladie, this is your trunk," Meryl said. "Do you have something to cut our bindings?"

I had nothing to cut our bindings. I didn't even have a spare tire.

Wait a second.

"I think I do have something," I said. I wiggled around until I could stick my hand in my back pocket. There, I found my new Robinson Bucks card. It sliced at my fingertips, but I managed to get it free. I started to saw at the ropes around my wrists.

"That mayor may be dumb, but he's dumb in a smart way," Meryl commented.

The four of us managed to get free with the card, but there was no emergency latch in the trunk, and no matter what we did, we couldn't get the trunk open.

Then, the car started to slow, and finally it stopped.

"Get ready for a counter-offensive, ladies," Lucy said.

"What does that mean?" Bridget asked.

"It means kick him in the balls and gouge his eyes out," Meryl explained.

The trunk opened, and Debbie stood over us with her gun pointed at our heads. Colin was there, too, and he had brought his axe. But at least our arms were free.

We climbed out of the trunk. I recognized where we were. It was not far from the Starfest meadow and very close to the cranberry bog. There were lots of places to run away to around here and more places to hide. There was no way they could kill us all at once. If I distracted them, the other three could escape.

It was worth a try.

I was about to do something brave, and I was probably going to die, but it was worth it if I could save Lucy, Bridget, and Meryl. They deserved to live.

But I was sorry to leave Spencer and Grandma. What would Spencer do without me? He would be despondent. He would grieve forever.

On the other hand, he would probably go back to his womanizing ways. He would probably date a different model every night like he used to before we were together.

Actually, he would probably like that. Models don't eat or talk, and they never get their heads stuck in blood pressure cuffs. And I had never once seen a model with a sex sheep stuck to their head.

Yep, I bet Spencer wouldn't even wait until my body was cold before he got out his Little Black Book, again.

Damn that Spencer!

How dare he keep his Little Black Book?

How dare he date models again?

I wasn't even dead, yet.

That was it. I wasn't going to die. I wasn't going to give Spencer that pleasure.

So, I wasn't going to sacrifice myself. Instead, I was going to figure out a distraction, and then the four of us were going to disarm the crazy killers. There. That was a good plan. I wish I could have communicated that to Lucy, Bridget, and Meryl so they would know the plan.

And what distraction? I needed a distraction. I looked up at the bright stars and asked the universe for a life-saving distraction, but the universe didn't answer.

"Debbie," Bridget said, waking me up from my inner dialogue. "Did you kill Pablo and the publisher, or was that your uncle?"

"What business is that of yours?" Debbie spat.

"Well, we kind of have a bet between us," Bridget

explained. "I think Colin killed them. You don't look very strong, and Colin's the serial killer. He's strong, and he knows how to plan murders. You just cook appetizers for a living. That's not very impressive."

Debbie waved her gun at Bridget. "Really? I can't plan? Who do you think spooked the bull? I poked him with the blunt side of the axe and away he went, and not one person saw me do it. How's that for planning and strength?"

"Impressive, darlin'," Lucy said. "I guess I win. I was sure you did that publisher in. A woman beating a big man to death on her own? Gloria Steinem would be proud of you."

Debbie smiled a crazy smile. Wow, you think you know people, and then they turn out to be loony tunes. That had happened a lot in my life.

"I beat him with a shovel," Debbie said. "I didn't even break a nail."

"I'm going to kill the girl with the glasses first," Colin said suddenly, pointing his axe at Bridget.

I had almost forgotten about Colin, but he definitely had not forgotten about us. He was eyeing Bridget with a sort of animal hunger while he handled the axe, like he was itching to use it. And I knew that he wouldn't hold back. After so many years, he wasn't going to be content with letting his niece do the killing. He wanted a turn with an axe.

Oh my God. This was it.

We were going to die in the middle of nowhere.

Distraction! Distraction! Come on, universe, give me one!

There was a loud creaking noise from my car and then the sex doll seemed to fart. It was long and slow and high-pitched. We watched as the doll began to actually move from side to side and finally, it rolled off the car and dropped to the ground with such force that it picked up momentum and began rolling down the hill.

"Huh, look at that," I said. "The NASA glue wore off. So much for safety in a meteor shower."

Suddenly, I realized that this was the distraction I had been waiting for. I screamed at the top of my lungs and launched my body at Debbie. Her gun went off, and a nearby tree branch fell to the ground.

Lucy karate-chopped Debbie's arm and she dropped the gun.

Lucy picked it up and started shooting it up at the sky. Meanwhile, Meryl jumped onto Colin's back and bit his shoulder like she hadn't eaten in months. He yelped and tried to hit her with his axe, but Bridget kicked him in the balls, and he dropped the axe.

Colin managed to shake Meryl off of him, and he ran into the trees.

A second later, there was a terrifying scream.

And then another one.

And then a few more.

They all came from Colin, and it didn't sound like he was doing all right.

Then, he was quiet.

The trees rustled, and the alligator appeared.

"Is that...?" Bridget asked.

"Colin's leg in that creature's mouth? Why, yes, it is," Lucy said.

"Uncle Colin!" Debbie cried.

It wasn't apple pie, but the alligator seemed happy with Colin's appendage. Just like that, we were heroes again.

"That's not a good way to die," I noted.

"It's good enough for the likes of him," Lucy said, and I couldn't argue with her.

"We felled two killers with the help of an endangered species," Meryl said, sounding amazed at our accomplishment. "They'll definitely name a street after us now."

"Pinky!" I heard, and Spencer appeared right behind the alligator.

He rushed over to me and gave me a bone-crushing hug.

"I was hunting the alligator, and suddenly the sex

doll came barreling down on us. And then I heard the gunshots. Are you all right?" he asked.

"Why?" I asked. "Are you disappointed? If I had died, you could date models again."

"Are you kidding me?"

"No, and why do you still have your Little Black Book?"

He arched an eyebrow. "I get the feeling that I came into this conversation late."

"Whatever," I said. "All I know is that I'm going to live a long time so you can never date a model again."

"Ouch, Pinky. That's harsh. I thought I could get a little action with a catalogue model for my birthday. At the very least."

I punched him in the arm. "Not funny."

"Who's joking?"

CHAPTER 17

And they all lived happily ever after. Why doesn't the minister or the rabbi or the priest ever say that? Have you ever wondered? They never do. Because the end of the wedding is actually a beginning, bubbeleh. A fabulous beginning, fresh and new with just the undigested wedding meal to deal with. After they break the glass or get the last blessing or throw the bouquet or whatever they do, they begin the long, sometimes difficult, journey to their happily ever after. It can be a fabulous adventure, dolly, or it can be an adventure full of kvetching. Sometimes it's both. But whatever it is, it's an adventure, a constant striving toward the happily ever after. This, for me, is the best possible part of the joining of two people in love.

— Lesson 17, Wedding Business Advice From
Your Grandma Zelda

The next week on Tuesday, after Grandma's Second Chancers Singles meeting, she, Spencer, and I ate a long, leisurely brunch in the kitchen.

Since we couldn't decide on sweet or savory, we had it all. And why not? We were celebrating being alive, and I was eating to dull the pain of having most of my hair cut off.

"It'll grow back, dolly," Grandma told me. "Here, have an olive. It'll make you feel better."

"My hair is three inches long. I look like a boy," I complained and ate the olive.

"You didn't look like a boy this morning," Spencer argued. "Not from my vantage point, in any case."

"You weren't looking at my head."

"Oh, you have a head too?" he joked and winked at me while he pinched my butt.

It turned out that Bird couldn't get the sex sheep off my head. The glue holding the sex doll to the roof of my car wasn't as strong as whatever the teenagers used to defile my once long locks.

"Pass the cheesecake," I said.

Spencer cut a slice and put it on my plate. I dug in and washed it down with some coffee.

"I guess the weird has returned," Spencer said,

like he was resigned to the fact. "We had a nice break, but it's obvious it's over now."

"Why?" I asked, interested. "Did something else happen?"

Spencer cut his waffle and dipped it into a pool of maple syrup. "Do you mean did someone else get killed? No, and thank goodness for that. I'm still filling out paperwork from Colin and Debbie's handiwork. Do you know how much paperwork there is with a serial killer case? And there are federal agents all over, looking for more bodies."

"Sister Cyril told me that Dave fell into one of the holes they dug, looking for bodies," Grandma said, chewing on a herring. "Dave went into his backyard, and down he went. Three feet."

"But I'm not even talking about that," Spencer said. "I'm talking about little things that prove that the weird has returned. I don't want to get into it, but let's just say that sex dolls riding on cars is just the start of it."

The front door opened. "Over here, Mayor," Grandma called.

The mayor appeared in the kitchen, and Grandma invited him to eat with us. He took a seat, and she offered him a plate.

"Thank you, Zelda," he said. "It's nice to know that someone is still civil to me. I've been getting a lot of punishment around town." He looked at Spencer. "You should do something about that, Chief."

Spencer put his hands up, like he was surrendering. "Hey, I'm not the one who set up a bogus monetary system in town."

"But I didn't know it was bogus," the mayor insisted. His voice cracked with emotion, and Grandma handed him a tomato, like that would fix it. "I was assured it was real. How did I know that nobody was going to get paid?"

Nobody got paid. Store owners were out a lot of money, and there was a rumor about starting a referendum to oust the mayor. I didn't believe that would ever happen. The mayor had never been in the slightest competent, but he had been our mayor for so many years that it was unthinkable that someone else would take his place.

"It'll work out," I told the mayor. "Uncle Harry has a rich friend who will visit this afternoon, fall in love with the town, and decide to reimburse all of the business owners."

"He will?" the mayor asked and looked at my grandmother for confirmation. She nodded at him. The mayor clapped his hands together. "Well, that's plucky news. Just plucky! Let's celebrate. Do you have any whole wheat toast, Zelda? I like whole wheat toast with jelly on it. That would hit the spot."

The door opened, and I heard Bird march in. She was smiling from ear to ear and stood by the refrigerator, like she was an actress on stage, about to give a soliloquy.

"Guess what!" she said. "Don't guess. I'll tell you. They dropped the lawsuit."

"We know," Spencer said.

Bird blinked, and her smile faded. "What? How do you know?"

"The owner of *Moo!* skipped town, and the crazy lactating women went with her," Spencer explained.

"Are you teasing me?" Bird asked and sat next to Grandma. She filled a mug with some coffee and took a sip.

"It turned out that the breast milk they were selling was actually cow's milk," Spencer told her. "There's a huge fraud case after them, and they're running from it."

The mayor coughed and sputtered. "What? No. No, no, no. I'm sure that it's breast milk. It has healing properties. It's very expensive."

"Sorry, Mayor," Spencer said. "It's cow's milk. Two-percent fat. The generic kind from Walley's. Margie found *Moo!*'s owner buying it by the case there, and then they tested the inventory, so, no more breast milk sold in Cannes."

"Hallelujah," I said and rubbed my eyes. They were finally better, but I wasn't taking any chances around lactating women.

"Well, this is a big weight off of my shoulders," Bird said. "We should celebrate. Do you have any sugar-free pudding, Zelda? That would hit the spot."

I served the mayor his toast and Bird her pudding. The door opened, again, and Lucy and Bridget came in.

"They're naming a street after us," Lucy announced.

"Lucy petitioned the Cannes Responsible Growth Commission," Bridget explained. "The street out by the dump will now be called Gladie Lucy Bridget Meryl Street."

"Really?" I asked.

They nodded and sat at the table.

Spencer kissed my cheek. "Congratulations, Pinky. Every time folks will go to the dump, they'll think of you."

"Pass the onion bagels, please," Bridget said. "A bagel with cream cheese would hit the spot."

"I could go for a slice of that coffeecake, Zelda," Lucy said. "That would hit my spot."

"I'd like to hit *your* spot," Spencer whispered in my ear.

"You already did this morning. Twice," I whispered back.

The door opened, and this time, Meryl came in. "Guess what!" she said.

"We know!" we answered in unison.

Everyone ate together for a long time, and when Spencer needed to leave to go back to work, he took my hand and pulled me into the parlor.

"I wanted to kiss you goodbye properly," he told me and pulled me close. He captured my mouth with his and kissed me like he meant it.

I kissed him back with as much passion.

"Don't forget the air conditioning repairman is coming at three o'clock," he told me after our lips were raw and chapped from kissing.

"You're not going to try and fix it?"

Spencer shook his head. "I don't think I'll have time for home repairs for a while, if you're going to be Miss Marple again."

"Only if someone gets murdered, and I would never hope for that."

Spencer arched an eyebrow. "Uh-huh."

"Do you have to leave so soon?" I asked. It felt good to be held and kissed, and the thought of doing it for the rest of the day was too much of a temptation.

"Sadly, I do. There was an alligator sighting by

the lake. At least now, I have the feds helping me. They need the alligator for evidence in the serial killer's case."

"I hope they don't hurt the alligator," I said. "I've gotten used to it."

"They're planning on giving it Ipecac and make him throw up Colin's remains. Then, he'll be returned to the San Diego Zoo."

He kissed me again and fondled my breast. "Listen," he said after a while. "Let's make a pact."

"Not another television pact. I don't want to watch any more *The Simpsons* reruns."

"Not that. And are you crazy? *The Simpsons* are the best. But anyway, our pact is never to keep anything from each other again. Last week, there was a lot of that, and I think we should base our relationship on open and honest communication. No more hiding, Pinky. No more hunting down killers after you tell me you're picking out tulle."

"I thought you didn't know what tulle is," I said.

"I looked it up. I'm not a caveman. So…deal? No more hiding?"

"Deal. I'll never keep anything from you again. From here on out, it's open and honest communication," I promised with my fingers crossed behind my back.

The End

*Continue the story with **Slay Misty for Me**, book two in the Matchmaker Marriage Mysteries. Sign up for my newsletter to be the first to know when it's released.*

https://bit.ly/2PzAhRx

AN AFFAIR TO
DISMEMBER

book one of the matchmaker mysteries series

elise sax

AN AFFAIR TO DISMEMBER

CHAPTER 1

When you first start out, you're going to ask people what they're looking for. This is a big mistake. Huge. They want the impossible. Every woman wants a Cary Grant with a thick wallet who doesn't mind if she's a few pounds overweight. Every man wants a floozy he can take home to Mom. See? Asking their opinion only leads to headaches you could die from. Take it from me, I've been doing this a lot of years. Nobody knows what they want. You have to size a person up and tell them what they want. It might take convincing, but you'll widen their horizons, and they'll thank you for it. Eventually. Remember, love can come from anywhere, usually where you least expect it. Tell them not to be afraid, even if it hits them on the head and hurts a lot at first. With enough time, any schlimazel can turn into a Cary Grant or a presentable floozy.

Lesson 22, Matchmaking Advice from Your
Grandma Zelda

The morning I found out about Randy Terns's murder, I was happily oblivious. I was too busy to care, trying to make heads or tails of my grandma's match-making business. Nobody actually mentioned the word "murder" that morning. I sort of stumbled onto the idea later on.

That Thursday I sat in my grandma's makeshift office in the attic of her sprawling Victorian house, buried under mounds of yellowed index cards and black and white Polaroid pictures. It was all part of Zelda's Matchmaking Services, a business I now co-owned at my grandma's insistence as her only living relative and what she called "a natural matchmaker if ever I saw one."

"Gladie Burger," she had told me over the phone three months before, urging me to move in with her, "you come from a long line of Burger women. Burger women are matchmaker women."

I was a Burger woman, but I had strong doubts about the matchmaker part. Besides, I couldn't decipher the business. It was stuck in the dark ages with no computer, let alone an Internet connection. Grandma fluctuated between staging workshops, running group meetings, hosting walk-ins, and just knowing when someone needed to be fixed up. "It's an intuitive thing," she explained.

I pushed aside a stack of cards, stirring up a black cloud of dust. I had been a matchmaker-in-training for three months, and I was no closer to matching any couples. To be truthful, I hadn't even tried. I wiped my dusty hands on my sweatpants and stared at the giant mound on her desk. "Grandma, I'm not a matchmaker," I said to her stapler. "I've never even had a successful relationship. I wouldn't know one if I saw one."

I had a sudden desire for fudge. I gave my stomach a squish and tugged at my elastic waistband. My grandmother was a notorious junk food addict, and I had slipped into her bad habits since I moved in with her. Hard to believe I was the same person who not even four months ago was a cashier in a trendy health food store in Los Angeles, the second-to-last job I had had in a more than ten-year string of jobs— which was probably why Grandma had twisted my arm to move to Cannes, California.

I decided against fudge and picked up an index card. It read: George Jackson, thirty-five years old. Next to the note, in Grandma's handwriting, was scribbled: Not a day less than forty-three; breath like someone died in his mouth. Halitosis George was looking for a stewardess, someone who looked like Jackie Kennedy and had a fondness for Studebakers. Whoa, Grandma kept some pretty old records. I needed to throw out ninety-five percent of the cards, but I didn't know which five percent to keep.

Putting down the card, I stared out the window, my favorite activity these days. What had I gotten myself into? I had no skills as a matchmaker. I was more of a temp agency kind of gal. Something where I wasn't in charge of other peoples' lives. My three-week stint as a wine cork inspector was more my speed.

A man and his German shepherd ran down the street. I checked my watch: 12:10 P.M. Right on time. I could always count on the habits of the neighbors. There was a regular stream of devoted dog walkers, joggers, and cyclists that passed the house on a daily basis. Not much changed here. The small mountain town was low on surprises. I tried to convince myself that was a good thing.

Stability was good. Commitment was good.

With sudden resolve, I took George Jackson's card and threw it in the wastebasket. "Bye, George. I hope you found love and an Altoid."

I tried another card. Sarah Johns. Nineteen years old. She had gotten first prize at the county fair for her blueberry pie, and she was looking for an honest man who didn't drink too much. My grandma had seen something more in her. Poor thing. Art school better than man, she had written in the margins.

I tossed the card, letting it float onto George. Matchmaking was no easy task. It wasn't all speed dating and online chat rooms. Lives were on the line. One false move and futures could be ruined.

The house across the street caught my attention. It had seen better days. A bunch of shingles were missing, leaving a big hole in the roof. I watched as the mailman stopped at the mailbox. He would arrive at Grandma's in twelve minutes. I could set my watch by him.

Across the street, the front door opened. An elderly woman stepped out and picked up her mail. She glanced at the letters and then stood staring at her front yard. Something was not quite right about the picture. I didn't have time to dwell on it, though. I had promised Grandma I would pick up lunch for us in town.

I grabbed my keys and hopped down the stairs. Outside, it was a typical Cannes, California, August day: blue sky, sunshine, and warm. Normally it didn't turn cool until October, or so I was told. My experience with the town was limited to summers visiting my grandmother when I was growing up. My mother refused to set foot in Cannes, but she had loved to send me off for a three-month vacation every year.

"Yoo-hoo! Gladie!" Grandma's high-pitched cry cut through the country quiet. She stood in the front yard, hovering over the gardener as he cut roses. The front yard was about half an acre of lawn and meticulously groomed plants, flowers, and trees. It was her pride and joy, and Grandma supervised the gardening with an obsession usually reserved for Johnny Depp or chocolate. I doubted she had ever picked up a spade in her life. "Yoo-hoo! Gladie!" she repeated, flapping her arm in the air, her crisp red Chanel knockoff suit bulging at the seams and the glittering array of diamonds on her fingers, wrists, and neck blinding me in the afternoon sun.

"I'm right here, Grandma." I jiggled the car keys to remind her of my lunch run.

"Jose, leave a few white ones for good luck and be careful with the shears," she told the gardener. "You don't want to lop off a finger." Jose shot her a panicked look and crossed himself.

Grandma walked as quickly as she could across the large lawn to the driveway. She had a grin plastered across her face and, no doubt, some juicy bit of news bursting to pop out of her mouth. Her smile dimmed only slightly when she got a good look at my state. I pulled up my baggy sweatpants. As usual, she was immaculately coiffed and made up, whereas my brown hair was standing up in all directions in a frantic frizz, and my eyelashes hadn't seen mascara in months. I didn't see much reason to dress up because I rarely left the attic, but standing next to Grandma, I was a little self-conscious about my attire. As a rule, her clothes were nicely tailored. I listened to the soft swish-swish of her pantyhose-covered thighs rubbing together as she approached. I wondered vaguely if the friction of her nylon stockings could cause them to burst into flames. I took a cowardly step backward, just in case.

"I'm so glad I caught you before you left," she said, a little out of breath from either her run or the excitement over the piece of gossip she was about to blurt out. While Grandma never left her property, she somehow knew everything going on in town.

"I didn't get much done," I said. "I can't figure out what to keep and what to toss. Should I throw out everything older than ten years?"

"Fine. Fine. Listen. Randy Terns is dead. They found him yesterday morning, deader than a doornail."

I racked my brain. Who was Randy Terns? Was he the new secretary of state? Really, I had to read a newspaper once in a while. What kind of responsible citizen was I?

"That's terrible," I muttered, a noncommittal edge to my voice in case Randy Terns was a war criminal or something.

"Yes, yes. Terrible. Terrible." Grandma waved her hands as if everything was terrible. The sky, the trees, my car— all terrible. She grabbed my arm in a viselike grip and pulled herself close to make sure that I heard every word. "I'm on Betty like white on rice to sell that old rundown excuse for a house. I'd love to get in some people who will fix it up. Look at me! I'm drooling over the thought of waking up, going out to get the paper, and not having to see that dreadful lawn across from my prize-winning roses." She made air quotes with her fingers when she said "lawn."

She turned to face the house across the street. "I bet you will be thrilled not to have to stare at that falling-down roof every day!"

Falling-down roof. My brain kicked into gear, and I recalled the woman standing by her mailbox. Randy and Betty Terns were the neighbors across the street. I'd never had much interaction with them. And now Randy was dead. Found yesterday morning, deader than a doornail.

I hate death. I'm scared it's contagious. At funerals, I feel my arteries start to harden. Medical shows on TV send me into neurotic fits. McDreamy or McSteamy, it doesn't matter— I only see my slow, agonizing death from a terrible disease. Like Ebola or flesh-eating bacteria. Or a drug-resistant superbug yeast infection. If I found out that poor Randy Terns died of a heart attack, it would only take five minutes or so for my chest pains to start.

"Betty said she would think about it," Grandma said with disgust. "Said she has a funeral to organize and a houseful of kids. Kids. Huh. The youngest is thirty-seven. Three of them still live at home. It's time to push those birdies out of the nest, I say."

She harrumphed loudly and kicked the cobblestoned driveway with her left Jimmy Choo. Gold-tipped. Very fancy.

"Five children. Why do people take things to extremes?" she continued. "Anyway, they come and go like they own the place, moving in and out whenever they want. They're holding on for dear life. A bunch of losers, the lot of them. I didn't make an index card for any of them." She looked at me expectantly, and I nodded vigorously in agreement, even though the most I saw of the "bunch of losers" these days were some faceless figures going to and from various cars.

Grandma patted a stray hair in place on her head and continued. "'Betty,' I told her, 'you could buy yourself a condo on the beach for cash and have enough left over to last your whole life if you sell now.' But she didn't have time for me. You know, Gladie, that house is one of the biggest on this street. And it's got a pool."

Grandma let out a big why-are-people-so-stupid sigh. Then she slapped her forehead. "I almost forgot! I have news about the house next to ours, too."

Geez. I really didn't want to hear that another neighbor had died. I would need therapy.

"Don't look at me like that, Gladie. It's good news. Jean, the real estate lady, told me there's been a bite on the house next door." She nodded to the house on my left. "A big bite. A whale bite. A… a… what's bigger than a whale? Whatever it is, it's one of those bites. Anyway, I can't talk about it yet. Might jinx it. Won't you be happy to have that house filled?"

I was only dimly aware that the house next door was empty and for sale, but my real estate ignorance would be sacrilegious to Grandma. The town was her business, and it was supposed to be mine now, too. A couple of speedwalkers made their way past us, distracting us from talk of houses and death.

"Daisy Scroggins," Grandma called out, flapping her arm at one of the speedwalkers. "You are the sweetest thing. How could I resist homemade chocolate chip cookies right out of the oven?"

The speedwalker, who I assumed was Daisy, stumbled in surprise. "How did you know I baked—" she started, but stopped herself midsentence. "I'll be back in fifteen minutes with a plateful, Zelda. It's the least I could do."

Grandma leaned into me. "Her daughter's wedding is next month," she whispered. "That was a tricky one, but in the end I convinced her to go for the plumber with one leg. She's never been happier, of course."

I had a familiar feeling of dread. Grandma's shoes were hard ones to fill. When the moment came, would I know to fix up someone with a one-legged plumber?

Jose let out a bloodcurdling scream. He jumped up from the rosebushes, clutching his hand. It grew redder by the second and started to drip.

"What did I tell you?" Grandma shook her head and clucked her tongue at him. "I cut off my finger," he yelled, his eyes wide with terror.

"No, you didn't," Grandma insisted. "It's just a

scratch. Good thing I told you to be careful. Let's go in, and I'll wash it." Jose followed Grandma into the house, holding out his hand in front of him as if it was a snake. I took that as my cue to hop in my car.

I drove a block before I realized I didn't know whether to go to Burger Boy or Chik'n Lik'n. I could have gone to Bernie's Rib Shack, my grandmother's favorite, but it was in a strip mall next to Weight Wonders, and I didn't want to face any dieters while getting an order of baby backs. I decided on Burger Boy because it was the closest and had the quickest drive-through.

My grandma's house was one of the oldest in town and located right in the center of the historic district on Cannes Boulevard near Main Street. The houses were a mishmash, most built in the haste of newfound money during the gold rush in the nineteenth century. The gold had run out pretty quickly, but people stayed on to enjoy the mountain views. The town had never grown much of anything, topping out at around four thousand people.

I drove south out of the historic district toward Orchard Road, where just beyond, hundreds of acres of apple and pear trees stood as a beacon to all those who came up the mountain for the town's famous pies.

Burger Boy was at the corner of Elm and Park, a few blocks before the orchard and across the street from Cannes Center Park. The park had been established about 150 years before in a wise attempt by the town's founders to preserve and protect the natural beauty of this little corner of Southern California paradise. It was a huge expanse of rolling hills, sagebrush, and eucalyptus trees. It used to have a lovely gazebo in the center with park benches all around, where they held weekly concerts and regular picnics. Then, in the late fifties, a few bored and prudish housewives caught some couples kissing on the park benches, and they lobbied to have the benches removed. It was decreed that the park should be used for brisk exercise and lounging on benches and in the gazebo would only lead to trouble and moral decay. The gazebo fell into disrepair. Gone were the kissing couples, and with them went the concerts and picnics. Today, brisk exercise was relegated to the historic district and the little park on Main Street. Cannes Center Park welcomed mostly skateboarders and teenagers searching for a little excitement in the bucolic small town.

Across the street from the park, Burger Boy had location, location, location and a killer dollar menu. It was a gold mine, a favorite of locals who did not particularly enjoy pie or tea.

An explosion rocked my car, jolting it forward a few feet before it slowed to normal. "Whoa, Nelly," I said, patting the dashboard. "No more car farts. I need you a while longer." I called them car farts. My mechanic called them a cataclysmic end to the catalytic converter. He had grumbled something to me about being one car fart away from total destruction and probable death, but I couldn't afford to fix it. Besides, it ran fine as far as I was concerned. It was a 1995 silver Cutlass Supreme, and I had gotten it for free when I worked at a used car lot for one month. I loved it, even though it had more rust than silver paint, and the interior was ripped, with foam poking out in tufts.

I rolled into the parking lot past a group of skateboarders hanging out in front, their skateboards leaning up against their legs as they packed away burgers, fries, and shakes. I followed the drive-through sign, winding through the parking lot toward the talking Burger Boy. I opened my window, and the smell of french fries hit me like nectar to the gods. Really, happiness was truly easy to acquire if you're honest with yourself. Maybe I could start eating right tomorrow.

Burger Boy's mouth was open in a big smile, and I yelled in its direction. "I would like two Burger Boy Big Burgers. No pickles. Extra cheese, please. Two large fries, and a Diet Coke."

There was a long silence, so I tried again. "I would like two Burger Boy Big Burgers, please!"

"Dude!" a voice shouted back at me.

"Yes, I would like two Burger Boy—"

"Dude! It doesn't work!" I leaned out the car window and tried to look into Burger Boy's mouth. The voice sounded much clearer than usual, but I still didn't understand what it was saying.

"Hey, dude. Like, the drive-through doesn't work, man." A skateboarder rolled up to my car, a shake still in one hand.

"Didn't you hear me? I've been yelling at you for, like, forever."

His shorts hung down well past his knees, and he wore a T-shirt that announced the price of beer bongs.

"Dude, I just thought of something," he went on. "If I didn't say anything, you would still be talking to the Burger Boy. So trippin'." He thought this was riotously funny and got so caught up in his own giggles that he didn't hear me when I said thank you and backed out of the drive-through lane.

I was disappointed about the drive-through, but I still had to get lunch. I was careful to lock up my car before I walked to the front door, passing the four skateboarders deep in conversation. Their attention was drawn to the sky.

"Dude, like, I think it's an eagle, man."

"No way, dude. It's an owl."

"I don't know, man. It's pretty big."

"Dude, it's been up there, like, you know, forever."

"Oh, man. It's been up there since last week at least. Maybe it thinks it's a tree or something."

"Cool." I looked up. Sure enough, an owl was perched on top of a telephone pole. I don't normally notice wildlife, don't know much about it, but two years before, I had had a job typing up a doctoral thesis on the endangered Madagascar red owl, and now I was staring up at one on a telephone pole at Burger Boy.

"Check it out. An eagle is up there," one of the skateboarders said, pointing it out to me.

"Actually, it's an owl," I explained.

"Oh, dude. She so burned you. I told you it was an owl." This came from the beer bong skateboarder, who I figured had held on to a few more brain cells than his friends.

"It's an owl from Madagascar," I informed them.

"Cool."

"It's not supposed to be here," I said. "It's highly endangered, and it's nocturnal. I don't understand what it's doing here."

They looked at me with empty stares. I had the strongest urge to knock on their foreheads to see if anyone was home.

Two things were certain: the four great geniuses were not about to help the endangered owl, and if I didn't help it, I would be responsible for driving the Madagascar red owl that much closer to extinction.

I sighed and dialed information on my cellphone. A minute later I was on the line with animal control, which proceeded to pass me to seven different offices around the state before I got to wildlife management. They said they couldn't get someone out here due to budget cuts and would I be so kind as to shoo it off or get it down.

"Get it down?" I asked.

"Yes. If it's too weak, just go up, grab it, carry it down, and take it over to animal control. We'll handle the rest."

"What if it has rabies or something?"

"Ma'am, birds don't get rabies. Just throw a shoe up there or something. It will fly away. It probably is enjoying the view."

The wildlife person hung up, and I stood there a moment, looking at my phone. Our tax dollars at work.

Sheesh.

"We have to shoo it down," I told the skateboarders.

"What? With our shoes, man?"

"You know, shoo. Like, shoo fly," I said. "But in this case, with our shoes. Throw your shoes up there to shoo it away. We have to make sure it's okay."

The beer bong guy was the first to take off his shoes, and the rest followed. I guessed he was kind of their leader. They threw their shoes up at the owl in unison, and I shielded myself from the onslaught of laceless, skull-embossed sneakers as they made their way back down to the ground.

I looked up, and sure enough, the owl was still there. He hadn't even blinked, which made me think he was in distress of some kind. Possibly more distress than what I was feeling at being stuck with a bunch of pothead skateboarders having to save an endangered species because my government wouldn't fund its budget properly.

"Okay. Well, that didn't work," I said. "So, one of you is going to have to go up there and get it down."

The guy who had thought the owl was an eagle looked at the telephone pole and whistled. "I don't know, dude. Can't you get electrocuted or something touching one of those poles?"

"No, no. This is a telephone pole. There's no danger with a telephone pole," I said. I was almost sure there was no danger with a telephone pole.

"I'm not much into climbing, man," said the beer

bong guy. And that seemed to clinch it for all of them. Without saying goodbye, they put on their shoes and rolled off into the park.

I waited a moment to see if some nice passerby would pass by, and then I kicked off my flip-flops, grabbed the pole, and started climbing. I got about halfway up before I got stuck on a metal doohickey and started screaming.

I was surprised and impressed that it only took about seven minutes for the police to come. Cannes was a very small town, and I didn't know it had so many police. Two squad cars and an unmarked car with a flashing light on its roof drove into the parking lot. I was amazed I had garnered so much attention.

"What the hell do you think you are doing?" one of the policemen yelled up at me.

"I was trying to get the owl," I shouted down with as much dignity as I could muster.

"Get down immediately!"

"I can't. I'm stuck on the metal doohickey." I was stuck. Stuck, and nothing was going to get me to move. I was sure any little movement would precipitate my plunge to earth. I sat on the metal ladder rungs, my legs wrapped around the pole in a death grip. My pant leg was punctured all the way through by the metal thing, my fear of heights had suddenly kicked in, and I was sweating so much that a nice slippery coat covered my body from head to toes.

I looked down at the policemen, who were deep in conversation. Four were in uniform, but one was dressed in plainclothes, an expensive suit.

A couple of minutes later I heard a siren and saw a giant hook-and-ladder fire truck come my way. Presto chango, they had a ladder against the pole, and a big fireman was climbing up to me.

"Don't worry, miss. I'll help you," he said.

"I was trying to get the owl for the wildlife management department. They have budget cuts," I told him.

"Happens all the time, miss. Come on. I got you." He put his arms around me and gave a little tug, and the ripping sound from my sweatpants could be heard across state lines. I pulled back, trying to minimize the tear, and my elastic waistband gave way as I fell upside down, my pants pulled down to my knees, my pink Victoria's Secret special three for fifteen dollars boy's-cut underpants out for everyone to see.

I heard snickering from the group below, which now included not just the police and the firemen but the entire staff of Burger Boy. In a moment of lunacy, I waved to them.

The fireman carried me over his shoulder down the ladder. Once on firm ground, I pulled up my pants.

"You have to get the owl. It's distressed and endangered," I told the fireman. He nodded and went back up to retrieve the bird.

The policeman in the suit approached me. He was tall. His thick, wavy, dark brown hair was perfectly cut and combed, his chin was shaved down to the last whisker, and despite a manly Gerard Butler kind of face, he looked like he was not averse to using moisturizer and the occasional clay mask. He had largish dark blue eyes and thick eyebrows. He arched one of those eyebrows as if he had a question.

"Yes?" I prompted.

"Cinderella?" he asked, his mouth forming a smile, revealing white teeth.

"Excuse me?"

"I was thinking you must be Cinderella." He held up my flip-flops. "I found these. They're yours, right?"

I put my hand out, and he placed the flip-flops in it. "I guess that makes me Prince Charming," he said.

Ew. Who did he think he was? I had just had a near-death experience.

He stood with his hands on his hips. His suit jacket was pulled back a bit, and I could see his badge and gun.

"I was trying to save the owl. It wasn't my idea. Wildlife management told me to do it," I said.

He smiled and cocked his head to the side. "I don't usually come out for these kinds of things, but I heard the call come out about a woman up a telephone pole and had to see it for myself. I'm not complaining, though, and neither is anybody else. Sergeant Brody over there says you have the finest rear end he's ever seen."

"Well, I'm sorry I wasn't up there longer to give everyone a better view."

"Don't worry about it. They all took photos with their cellphones," he said.

A deep heat crawled up my face, and my ears

burned. He studied me a second. "Hey, don't feel bad," he said, a smirk growing on his perfectly shaved face. "The town has cut back our overtime allowance, so the men have been pretty down. You just made everyone's day. I heard one guy say he hasn't felt this alive in twenty years."

One of the firemen approached us with the owl in his hands. "I got your owl," he said. He tapped it, making a hollow sound. "Plastic. It was put up there to scare away the pigeons so they wouldn't crap all over Burger Boy. I took it down so we don't have to go through this again. Although"— he winked at me— "I wouldn't mind the experience."

"But it looked so real," I moaned. Prince Charming took the owl from the fireman.

"Here," he said, presenting it to me. "You should have it."

"Thanks, but no thanks." I walked to my car and opened the door with a loud creak. Prince Charming was on my heels. He threw the owl behind me onto the backseat.

"Think of it as a souvenir."

I felt I needed to explain myself to him, and I hated myself for it. "I was just trying to be proactive."

"You were being a Good Samaritan," he said.

"I'm not like this normally." He gave me another annoying little smirk.

"I'm thinking there isn't much normal in your normally."

I gave him a sufficiently snotty look back and

started the car. "I don't think you're Prince Charming at all," I said.

He smiled from ear to ear. "Nice car." The Cutlass chose that moment to let rip its biggest car fart ever. I tried to retain my dignity, although I was guessing it was a little late for that. Besides, how dare he make fun of my only means of transportation? I was about to send back a zinger when he patted the roof and turned on his heel.

"Bye, Pinkie," he called, waving as he walked.

I took a long, healing breath. The day had been a big lesson for me. I would never wear elastic-waist pants again.

DIE

NOON

book one of the goodnight mysteries series

elise sax

DIE NOON
PART I: MATILDA MOVES IN AND FINDS A FEW SURPRISES

Goodnight Gazette Enters Uncertain Era
By Silas Miller

The new owner and publisher of the Goodnight Gazette, Matilda Dare, arrived in town today from California. She drove here in a beat-up Nissan Altima with no front bumper, a result of her running into a house back home. Ms. Dare has no experience in journalism and has never been to New Mexico before. She inherited the Gazette, along with its headquarters, which is housed in a prominent, historical compound home in the hills above the Goodnight UFOs shop and next to the Friends of Daisy the Giraffe Home for Abused Wildlife.

The former owner and publisher of the Gazette, Chris Simmons, died two weeks ago from an allergic reaction to a hornet sting while walking his dogs in the forest behind the house. Ms. Dare also inherited the dogs.

When asked if she would continue the newspaper or if she would shutter it, Ms. Dare responded: "What? I have a newspaper? What?"

The Goodnight Gazette won the Southwest Watchdog award five years in a row. It's a treasured fixture in the troubled town of Goodnight. Townspeople have been up in arms at the prospect of losing the Gazette. "If that woman shuts you down, I'll tase her," Patrolwoman Wendy Ackerman told this reporter at the Goodnight Diner. "No Californian can come here and tell us how to live."

Derek from Goodnight Fly Fishing Tours discussed his consternation about the newspaper's new owner. "What am I going to do about my advertising? I'll get a refund, right?" he asked over his breakfast of green chili eggs and sourdough toast.

This reporter will update our readers on the future of our paper, if Ms. Dare doesn't close it before he gets the chance. As for rumors that Matilda Dare is insane, calls to her hometown refuted them.

"No, she's not crazy," Gladys Burger, Ms. Dare's friend, insisted. "I mean, yes, she was locked up in a rubber room and shackled to a bed, but it was a mistake. She's as sane as I am."

In addition to being the town's matchmaker, Ms. Burger once found a severed head in a lobster tank, and she claims that she can predict the weather.

CHAPTER 1

My name's Matilda Dare, and I might see dead people. I mean, after they're buried and gone. I also have a problem with encountering more than my fair share of killers.

I didn't know any of that when I started my new life in Goodnight, New Mexico. I had only had one up close and personal killer up until that point, and I may or may not have brought a dead woman back to life. But boy, was that about to change.

I had left my old life behind two weeks ago, and I was now the owner of a large house, which included the headquarters of the Goodnight Gazette, two ancient dogs, and enough money to fix the plumbing and electricity and keep the paper running for three months. After that, I was going to have to sell pencils in town to survive.

But, I'm an optimist. So, after I arrived in town and was greeted by the four-person staff of the Goodnight Gazette like I was goose-stepping down the Champs Élysées and they were the French resistance, they informed me that I now owned the place, which was headquartered in my house, I heard myself say, "I plan on making a go of the paper," which surprised the hell out of me. The newspaper was totally unexpected, but it answered the question of what I was going to do in New Mexico. It's always good to know what one is going to do when starting a new life.

"Yeah? You're going to make a go?" Silas Miller, the head reporter, challenged me, while I still held the handle of my suitcase in my hand. "Do you know that the Gazette has never made a profit?"

"Nothing in Goodnight makes a profit," Klee Johnson, the managing editor, added.

"The diner does pretty well," Jack the paperboy said.

"That's true," Klee said. "I do love their smoked trout hash."

"Best green chili in town," Silas agreed. "But nothing else makes money here."

"How does the paper stay in business?" I asked. Klee shrugged, and it set off a wave of shoulders rising. "Well, that doesn't matter," I announced and broke out into panic-induced hives. "I believe in the importance of a free press in a democracy. So, this will be a go."

I made a silent prayer that there would be a major earthquake, which would create a large crevice that would open in the earth to swallow me up. But then I remembered that I wasn't in California anymore. So, I prayed for a fire. But God wasn't cooperating. Instead of sending me a natural disaster, he sent me a financial disaster.

Luckily, just then the paper got a call about a possible UFO sighting over the fracking fields west of town, and the focus moved from me to Martians. Then, I found my room, left to me from a dead relative I never knew I had, and took four Xanax while I scrubbed and cleaned and organized before I went to bed with a couple tiny bottles of booze, which I had taken from the mini fridge at a motel in Phoenix on my way to Goodnight.

But, of course, I didn't sleep. I hadn't slept since I was a teenager. I was hoping that the fresh, mountain air would help, but it didn't. Instead, in addition to not being able to sleep, I couldn't seem to get a lungful of air, no matter how much I tried.

Later, Klee told me that I had altitude sickness and that it would go away in a couple of months. "If you last that long," she added, like she wasn't at all convinced.

She had warmed up since then. In my experience, neat freak insomniacs are hard to love, but we're great landlords. In two weeks, I had scrubbed the living quarters from the floors up to the ceilings and planted flowers in the courtyard. Klee approved. She also liked that I left the Gazette in her hands. It was her territory, and I knew better than to invade.

Little did she know that I planned on victory by attrition, earning my ownership with tiny, imperceptible steps. I was an all or nothing kind of person, but I always seemed to choose all instead of nothing.

In my zeal and tendency to lean toward the extremes, I usually failed in my efforts. But not this time. This time, I was determined to live happily ever after. Especially after what I had gone through back in California.

That's why I sat in on the morning editorial meeting for the first time that Monday, and that's how it all started. My new life. And love, too. If I had been satisfied to leave well enough alone and leave journalism for the journalists, it might have all turned out differently. There would have been no adventures. I would never have found my place. And the rest. Well, the rest would have happened, but I would have never known about it.

The house was made of mud plaster, one-story cut into a square of four wings with a courtyard in the middle. The Gazette's offices were in the front section of the house. I walked in past Klee's desk and sat by the wall, next to two desks that were pushed together. Those belonged to Silas and the junior reporter, Jimmy Sanchez, a thin young man who was convinced that he was better than all this and was destined to make it to The Washington Post. The paperboy was in school and so wasn't at the meeting.

"What're you doing here?" Silas demanded. "Figuring out what to do with this space when you shut us down?"

As far as I could tell, Silas only had one suit, which he wore every day. It was a greenish brown with a stain on the lapel. He had two button-down shirts, both short-sleeved. I figured they used to be white, but that ship sailed a long time ago. His tie was pulled loose so that his top shirt button could rest undone. He was sitting with his legs outstretched, resting on his desk, crossed at the ankle, giving me a good look at the bottoms of his shoes. He wore old-fashioned, brown Hush Puppies slip-ons, and the soles were nearly worn through. His desk was piled high with paper with a narrow tunnel for him and his computer.

Jimmy's desk was bare, with just a computer and not a scrap of paper. On his skinny frame, he wore a tight black suit, which was a couple of inches too short. Klee looked fabulous in flowy slacks and a hand-painted tunic, chunky jewelry, and a handwoven scarf that wound around her neck three times. She was a beautiful older woman with thick, long black hair. Her desk was covered in organization boxes, plastic shelves, and a large phone with a shoulder rest attached to the handset.

"I'm not going to shut you down," I told Silas for the millionth time. I so wanted to shut them down. The paper was like an albatross around my neck. I had no idea about how to run a newspaper or journalism in general, and I had even less of an idea how to make it profitable. "I'm here to learn. And I'm here to help."

Silas's mouth dropped open before it turned into a smile. "You want to help? Hear that Klee? I think we can get some work for the boss. What do you think?"

"I've got the reopening of the Goodnight Community Pool at nine," Klee said, handing me a press release. "How about three hundred words?"

"What? You want me to write?" I asked.

"I heard that you have three PnDs," she said. I did. They were in Floral Management, Bowling Industry Technology, and Leisure Studies. None of them required writing. And three hundred words? How long was that? Twenty pages? I had no idea. But I did know I couldn't write twenty pages.

"Three hundred words. No problem," I said, skimming the one-paragraph announcement about the pool.

"Jimmy, get the woman a glass of water," Silas ordered. "The boss looks like she's going to pass out or have a stroke. One or the other."

Jimmy scowled and went to the water cooler. "I'm fine," I lied.

"Don't worry. I'll walk you through it," Silas said,

surprising me. "If we leave soon, we'll have an hour at the diner before you have to be at the pool, and I'll give you the rundown on how to be a reporter."

Klee handed out the assignments. Jimmy was going to take the "if it bleeds, it leads" beat, and Silas had a list of about ten stories to cover, including a big investigative piece on a petroleum company and water rights.

We headed out at about a quarter to eight, and I followed Silas to the diner in my Altima. I was both nervous and excited about my assignment. I enjoyed tackling something new, but I wished I had more time to learn how to do it.

The diner was a centerpiece in town, but since I had been stuck cleaning at home, I had never eaten there. It was located in the plaza, wedged in between the Goodnight Hat Shop and the Goodnight Porcelain Cat Shop.

I parked behind Silas's old, gold, four-door Cavalier on the street in front of the diner and walked in with him. He opened the door, which made a ringing sound, and walked in, not bothering to hold it open for me. The diner had booths all along the walls and about five round tables in the center. The kitchen was at the back of the diner with a long open cutout where the cook put the finished meals to be picked up. Everything was clean, but dingy.

The diner was packed with working men, and they all turned to look at me when I entered. Silas waved at a woman about my age and took a seat in a booth by the window. "Adele, get the boss a menu. She'll probably want one."

I sat down and took the menu from Adele. "It's about time you came in," she said to me. "Nearly everyone in this town is a regular. What're you doing up in that house? Eating cereal? Nobody can survive on cereal. You're in Goodnight, now, sweetie. You need eggs. You need tortillas. I know what you need." She took the menu from me before I had a chance to look at it. "I'm Adele. I know everything that goes on in Goodnight. I know all about your husband in San Quentin, for example. So, you come to me if you need anything. We don't get a lot of people moving into Goodnight, you know. Not with our bad giraffe karma. And then there's the nuclear waste. And the fracking's not fabulous." She said the last bit in a whisper, eyeing the two tables full of men wearing uniforms with a petroleum company's logo on them.

"I'm glad a single woman moved in. Not many of us single gals around these parts," she continued, touching her hair. "I'm a widow, myself."

"I'm sorry for your loss. That's tough," I said. I

was in the middle of a divorce to a man who put me away in a rubber room and later tried to kill me, but I thwarted his plans and conked him over the head and turned him in to the police.

Marriage is complicated.

"Doubly tough since I killed him," Adele said, wiping some lipstick off of her front teeth.

"Excuse me?"

"It's not what you think. It wasn't my fault."

"So, you what? Fed him too much saturated fat?"

"Oh, no. The man ate chicken fried steak every day of his life and had arteries you could drive a truck through. I shot him through the head. That's how he died. But it wasn't my fault."

"Are you done?" Silas asked, irritated. "Are you going to branch off into period talk? Waxing? Natural mineral cosmetics? All day with women it's yap, yap, yap."

"All that meanness is going to eat you from the inside out," Adele spat at Silas. "You're a mean, mean man. I should have shot *you* in the head. Don't worry, you'll get your food soon enough. Not that you couldn't survive skipping a few breakfasts."

"We have work to do," Silas countered. "The press is under attack. We will not be silenced," he bellowed.

Adele hit him hard over the head with the menu and walked to the kitchen.

Silas leaned forward and counted on his fingers. "Who, what, where, how, and why. Can you remember that?"

I nodded.

"No! You're not going to remember that. You're in the journalism game now, boss. Write down everything. *Everything*. You get me?"

I nodded.

"No!" he yelled, again. "I gave you a reporter's notebook. Get it out, *now*. A reporter is always writing in their notebook. Facts. Write the facts. So, what're you going to write?"

I pulled the reporter's notebook out of my purse. "Everything," I said.

"Good girl. Good boss. Adele! What does a man have to do to get coffee in this dump?"

"A man could ask nicely," she said and brought the coffee over.

"So, what do I write about at the pool? Do I just watch or should I ask questions?" I asked Silas.

"You watch. You ask questions. And when you've got the who, what, where, how, and why figured out, you leave. Then, you write it down in three-hundred words. Lead sentence is the most important. Lead paragraph, second important, until you get down to the I-don't-give-a-fuck part. Got me, boss?"

"You keep using that boss word, but I don't think you know what it means."

Silas punched me in the arm and laughed. "You're all right, boss."

Adele put two plates down on our table. "Smoked trout hash with green chilies and sourdough toast," she announced. "So good, you'll slap your mama."

I drove the three blocks to the Goodnight rec center. I was fine when I was sitting down, but every time I took a step, I would gasp for air. Goodnight was set up a lot like Santa Fe with old, squat buildings on short streets around a plaza, but the comparisons ended there. Santa Fe was a rich, vibrant city full of artists. Goodnight was a dying town with a nuclear fallout problem.

Nuclear waste or not, breathing or not, I was feeling optimistic. I was on my way to my first reporting assignment, and it made me feel like I was in control, helping the Gazette become profitable so that my new life could be sustainable. Still, my one-minute journalism class from Silas wasn't filling me with self-confidence.

"Who, what, where…" I repeated, as I parked on the street. Damn it. I had already forgotten the rest. A woman knocked on the passenger window, and I stepped out of the car.

"Are you from the sheriff's department?" she asked.

"No. I'm with the Gazette."

"Oh, that must be why you're not driving a sheriff's car. Do you have a gun?" she asked, hopefully. I shook my head. "Oh, well. Mabel has a cattle prod. Normally that would do it, but Norton's got a few more pounds on him than a bull."

"I'm here for the pool reopening?" I said like a question.

"Me, too," she said walking back into the rec center. I followed her. "I'm Nora. I work over at Goodnight Bank. Are you the crazy woman who bought old man Simmons' house?"

"I inherited it. He was some kind of distant cousin. And I'm not really crazy. My husband gaslighted me and put me away."

"I heard you ate a live lizard."

"What?"

It was a small rec center, and we walked through it to the outside where there was a pool and about twenty people standing around holding pool noodles and assorted pool equipment. Everyone was focused on a fracas by the diving board. A tall woman around sixty-years old with a long, narrow nose was pointing a cattle prod at an enormous man wearing a Speedo bathing suit and holding a large, inflatable duck.

"This is a family place!" she yelled at him.

"That's Mabel," Nora told me. "And that's Norton, the one with the duck, and the cleavage."

"I have a family. I'm a family man, and I want to swim," Norton countered.

I took my reporter's notebook and a pen out of my purse. *What, where, when, how, and why*, I reminded myself. "Is Mabel in charge of the pool?" I asked Nora.

"And the rec center and the library and half of the town."

"Here I go," I muttered and clicked my pen, holding it over my notebook. I walked toward Mabel, making sure to keep a safe distance away from her cattle prod. "Hello. I'm Matilda Dare from the Goodnight Gazette. Can you tell me about the pool reopening? Whoa!"

Standing next to Mabel, I got my first frontal look at Norton. The view from the back had been impressive enough, but the front had a whole lot happening.

"See? See?" Mabel shrieked at Norton. "Even the loony girl is shocked by the sight of you. Now, put a top on or you have to go."

"I'm a man, Mabel. And I need to feel free. I like the water to touch my body. My skin. It's a sensory thing. Are you trying to deprive me of my sensories?"

"But you have boobs!" she yelled. She was right. He had boobs. They weren't the expected man boobs situation of most large men. They were *boobs*. Beautiful D-cup breasts. I was a B-cup, and my left boob was bigger than my right. But Norton had it all going on. He could have been a boob model, if there was such a thing as boob models and if no one minded the thick patch of black hair on them.

"Body shamer!" he yelled. "Sensory depriver! I gotta be me! I gotta be me!"

"This is a family pool! It's not the Playboy Mansion!" she countered.

"My body needs total immersion in the water without fabric getting in the way. Fascist!"

"Pervert!"

"Commie!"

"Degenerate!"

"Brown shirt!"

"Weirdo!"

"Uptight middle manager!"

It was a boob standoff. It was like a protest at a nude beach but with a twist. What would Bob Woodward do in these circumstances? Would he continue the interview? I was pretty sure he would.

"Did you enlarge the pool, or was it just replastered?" I asked Mabel, averting my eyes from Norton's cleavage, which was no easy task. She didn't answer, distracted by movement near the door to the rec center.

I looked over, too. The sheriff had arrived with a deputy. He was a very tall man and big, but not like Norton. Like John Wayne. He was wearing jeans, a blue button-down, boots, a cowboy hat, and a big, gold sheriff's star on his chest. His eyes flicked to me and then to Mabel, who was waving him over. The deputy with him was a young, slim woman weighted down by her uniform and a heavily laden utility belt. But I didn't look much at the deputy. My eyes were fixed solely on the sheriff.

Here's the thing. I never wanted another man in my life. Never. I had had a man, a husband, and he turned out to be a killer. He also married me in order to get an inheritance and put me away in a funny farm. So, obviously my radar wasn't good about men. If I liked a man, it probably meant that he was a lying, no account murderer. Or worse.

Yes, maybe I had trust issues. Maybe I had been burned once and should have let it go, and whatever the universe threw my way, I should have welcomed with open arms. But my husband was a killer! He married me to get an inheritance, and he gaslighted me and sent me off to a funny farm!

So, damned right I had trust issues. All kinds of trust issues.

If he had a penis and was good-looking, I couldn't possibly trust him.

And guess what. The sheriff was good-looking, and he had a penis. I was sure of it. And when our eyes met for only a fraction of a second, I knew I was doomed. Damned chemistry. It's every woman's enemy.

But I was going to be strong. I was going to resist chemistry. So, I focused on Norton's boobs.

"Hey there, Amos," Mabel said to the sheriff. "I'm trying to reopen the pool, and Norton insists on being Bo Derek."

Amos the sheriff nodded at Norton. "Mornin'," he said. His voice was deep and gravelly, and I could feel one of my ovaries spur into action, shoving an egg down my fallopian tube in hopes of getting some Amos action.

Traitorous ovaries. I couldn't trust them, either.

"Amos, I like the feel of the water on my body. It's a sensory thing. You gotta cook, and I gotta let my body be free," Norton told him. Amos nodded, again.

"But look, Amos! Look!" Mabel sputtered, gesturing toward Norton's gorgeous, hairy rack.

"Freedom!" Norton yelled, raising a hand in the air and making his right boob jiggle like twenty pounds of Jell-O.

"For the love of Pete," Mabel groaned.

The crowd was growing restless. It was a hot summer's day, and the water looked inviting.

"We can do this a couple of ways," Amos said, calmly. His cowboy hat was pushed low over his face. I knew that his eyes were a smoldering dark brown that a woman could get lost in, but for the moment, his face was downturned, thankfully hiding his eyes. "You can do what I tell you to do."

"So, actually you mean we can do this one way," Norton said. The sheriff lifted his head and shot Norton a look. Totally John Wayne. Norton swallowed. "Fine."

Mabel smiled. "Thank you, Amos."

Amos nodded at her. He didn't talk much, and it suited him. With so much swagger and hotness, he didn't need to say a word.

"I'll get my shirt," Norton said.

Norton moved to get his shirt. I stepped out of his way at the precise moment he dropped his inflatable duck. My foot landed on the duck, and I went flying. My survival instinct kicked in, and I grabbed for support, determined not to fall.

Unfortunately, the closest thing to grab onto was

Norton's boobs. I grabbed on with both hands. "I'm sorry," I cried and pushed away from him, horrified.

"No problem," he said and then he stepped on the duck, too, and he lost his balance. He teetered, trying not to fall, but he was going over, and he was going over on me. I put my hands out to stop him and whacked him hard in the man-boobs.

They were like magnets, and I was helpless not to touch, hit, or squeeze them. It was like not trying to think of something and then thinking of it.

Norton yelped, unable to regain his balance. "Save yourself!" he yelled, and then he was on me, and we both went over, inaugurating the reopened pool.

I hit the water on my back with Norton's chest smothering my face. As we went down, down, down to the bottom of the deep end, I thought: *So this is how I'm going to die. Drowned under an enormous man in a Speedo.*

I willed him to get off me, but he was struggling, too, and it dawned on me that maybe his rubber duck was not a toy but a flotation device and he didn't know how to swim. Lying on my back in the deep end, I wasn't having a whole lot of positive thoughts flash through my mind. I had hoped that he would float up, but there wasn't that much floating going on. I had exhaled on impact, and now the last of my oxygen was going fast.

Just as I was giving up hope, Norton flew off me,

and a second later, a strong hand grabbed onto my arm and yanked me up out of the water. The sheriff had saved me, picking me up and letting me down gently at his feet on the deck.

I sat on the cement like a wet dishrag, dripping all over the sheriff's boots. Norton climbed out of the pool and looked down on me with concern.

"I guess you're right, Mabel," he said. "I'm too distracting shirtless. She couldn't keep her hands off me."

"I told you," she said, looking down at me, too. "She went after you like you were potato salad on the Fourth of July."

"She squeezed me like she was making lemonade."

"Like she was honking in traffic."

"Like she was picking apples."

"Are you okay, honey? You don't need CPR, do you?" Mabel asked me.

"I…didn't…I, mean…I…oh, forget it," I said and kept dripping.

"It's fine," Norton bellowed, as if I had lost my hearing. "You just took in some chlorinated water. You might have diarrhea later, but it'll pass. Ha! Get it? Pass?" I didn't answer. "I don't think she hears me. You know, I heard she dressed as a bunny rabbit and ate only carrots for a month." He inspected me, like he was looking for traces of leftover bunny.

"I heard she thought she was Wonder Woman and lassoed a high school track and field team at their practice," Mabel said.

Boy, journalism was a bitch.

ABOUT THE AUTHOR

Elise Sax writes hilarious happy endings. She worked as a journalist, mostly in Paris, France for many years but always wanted to write fiction. Finally, she decided to go for her dream and write a novel. She was thrilled when *An Affair to Dismember*, the first in the *Matchmaker Mysteries* series, was sold at auction.

Elise is an overwhelmed single mother of two boys in Southern California. She's an avid traveler, a swing dancer, an occasional piano player, and an online shopping junkie.

Friend her on Facebook: facebook.com/ei.sax.9
Send her an email: elisesax@gmail.com
You can also visit her website: elisesax.com
And sign up for her newsletter to know about new releases and sales: https://bit.ly/2PzAhRx

Printed in Great Britain
by Amazon